SILENT FALLS

His eyes watched the aftermath with horror, his hands trembled violently. The nauseating stench overwhelmed his nose, the rotting flesh mixed with mud turned his stomach. Blood painted the small village walls, etching out words of desperation. The young boy stepped over freshly torn limbs, faces frozen in fear. Snatching the boy's leg, the corpse shifted, moaning in agony. Max quickly jumped away, running as fast as he could. His heart pounded loudly, sweat poured off his face in the summer heat. The fountain laid ahead, cracked and shattered. Her beautiful golden hair, stained with blood laid against the fountain, her eyes devoid of life. The young boy darted towards her, shaking his mother's shoulders. The hole in the chest was wide and deep, exposing her insides, her heart laid in the dirt, still beating. The hot tears busted at the seams of his eyes rushing like waterfalls. His hands held tightly to her pale arms, weeping loudly. The light footsteps broke his weeping, his eyes cautious as he peered through the thick fog. His body relaxed, recognizing the figure, his eyes lit up. Max raised up, darting towards the man. "Dad!", his voice called out, relieved to see him alive. The man continued towards Max; his emerald eyes full of hope. Max reached his arms around the man's waist. The cold skin felt unnatural on his face, almost unwelcoming. The man's slimy hand reached around the young boy's body. The cold sweat began to drip his face, the feeling of safety stripped away quickly. Max pulled away, stumbling to the ground. Clawing at the dirt, his legs pulled towards the monster. Its massive fleshly tendrils pressed down on Max, holding the boy down. The demonic laugh erupted around him, taunting his failed attempts at escape.

Flesh ripped; blood began to pour at the seams of his side. The young boy held on tightly, his fingernails filled with dirt. His hands let go, sliding towards his oppressor. Max turned to face it, it's grotesque body large in size. It rose his massive hands, roaring loudly. The high-pitched screams filled the sound. Sweat poured from his face, the sheets drenched. The alarm clock rang out, he rubbed his eyes. The scar on his waist, faint and stitched. Light peered through the cracked shades, its rays blinding his tired, blue eyes. Rows of suits lined the closet, his hands sliding through hangers. The dimly grey suit jacket pulled at his hands, sliding off the hanger. He slipped the dark navy tie onto his neck, sighing quietly. The black dress pants complimented his white undershirt, his shoes shined dully on his feet as he exited the house. His brown hair blew softly in the wind, his hand struggling to comb it back down. The street was filled with citizens, buzzing along the sidewalks. As he walked through the crowded street, he waved, the people cheered, eager to get closer to Max. Smiling dimly, he continued his trek towards the park. The breeze blowing through the autumn trees, bringing a crisp feeling to his warm face. The Park was quiet, empty but surreal. The large tree ominously shadowed him, the cool sun leaving his skin, bringing the chilly breeze to his body. Max stepped up to the tree, reaching for his phone. The beeping chimed quietly, filling the screen with missed calls. Clicking quickly, he glanced around, then peered down at the screen. Ringing, the phone vibrated as he tapped his foot against the soft ground rapidly, surveying his surroundings. The voice was loud, ringing loudly through the speaker of the phone. "Hello? What you need, my man?", Max paused, glancing around one final time. "Open the door.", The man quickly responded, his tone playful. "Password, please!", Max furiously tapped his shoe, sighing in embarrassment. "Open the door, Demon slayer.", The irritated tone increased, his teeth gritted. The call ended; his phone slid back into his pant pocket. Max quickly darted his eyes to the side of him, peering at the path. Its trunk shifted mechanically, the bark pulled itself back, leaving the dark entrance to the bright sun. Max darted inside, the door shifted behind him, closing. The darkness filled his vision, as he stood still. Lowering, the metallic floor shifted, it's mechanical gears creaking loudly. The grey light came to his vision, doors creaked and slid open revealing the metallic walls. Max stepped out of the elevator, covering his eyes to the blinding light. Machinery whirled silently; blue lights blinked rapidly as he entered the laboratory. "I see someone is having a not-so wonderful morning.", a voice echoed from the desk. A cup of coffee sat on top, steam rolling out of the cup. His shaven beard was neatly dressed, his amber eyes full of excitement. Leaning back in the chair, he stared down at the tan folder, enveloped in its contents. "Any progress from yesterday's breakthrough?", Max asked, his voice firm. He leaned against the wall, his eyes flickering towards the man. "Well, it seems the frame is holding up the initial test we ran yesterday." Tom paused, his eyes peering at the folder. "But, good news? Bad news? I want to hear it, Tom.", Max snapped back, sighing quietly. Tom sat forward; his face serious. "But there is no energy source on this god-forsaken planet to sustain the reaction.", Tom sat the folder on the desk, pushing his glasses up. "I don't have enough time, Max.", Tom explained. Max stepped forward, hands trembling in anger. "We.", he paused, raising his head to meet Tom's eyes. "We don't have any more time!", Max shouted, his hands waved wildly in the air. "The invasion is imminent. I can't keep prolonging the inevitable destruction of my city with peace talks!", His voice strained, his head throbbed. "Emperor Marcus is a power-hungry individual. If we don't find a solution to our energy problem, then all of our work will be lost, including our lives.", Max began to pace across the room, muttering quietly. "Max, my man." Tom spoke, bringing Max back to reality. "There is hope, I just need more time. The gateway to the Aether will be open, and soon our people can reside there in harmony. I promise this, our work will not go in vain.", Max turned away, stepping towards the containment room. It's tinted glass windows revealing the grey portal frame inside. "I know. I apologize for the yelling.", Max turned away from the window, his eyes wet. "Not the tears man! We're a team.", Tom laughed, shaking Max's hand. Max laughed, glancing down at his golden watch. "Oh,

I suppose I'm a little late for that conference.", Max sighed, giving a quick wave at Tom before exiting the lab. The small elevator creaked, the metallic doors closing as sunlight peered in the small windows. The wooden trunk swung open as Max quickly headed across the trail, fixing his tie. The bright sun hung over his head, beaming down on the trees. Max leaned forward checking the sides of the street before exiting the trail. He pulled the leaf off his jacket, briskly walking towards the conference. The city's tall buildings rose endlessly towards the sky, touching the highest of clouds. Max's eyes darted towards his watch, "*5 minutes late, I can handle the heat.*"; His legs hopped up the concrete stairs, the elegant building sparkled in the sunlight. It's quartz outline shimmered to his eyes. Swinging the door open, he entered quietly, the table filled with business suits and elegant dresses. Their eyes darted towards the door, his smile trying to appease their impatience. "I deeply apologize that I am fashionably late. The waitress simply couldn't get my name right.", The conference chuckled a small laugh, before returning to their stone-like expressions. Sitting down in the squeaky chair, he glanced at the documents below him. "Mr. Salem.", Max announced, his eyes scanning the papers. A man in the back stood up, his extensively large stature made the room whisper in astonishment. His dark brown eyes met Max with a fierce look of determination. "Your company wants forty-percent of the governmental shares? That's quite a bit of a fortune. ` `, The man smiled wide, his voice boomed across the room. "Yes, I do, I'll be willing to provide compensation if requested.", Max looked puzzled, "Compensation? May you elaborate on that, Mr. Salem?", His head tilted, he raised his eyebrows up. "My company provides protection, weaponry, and highly experimental technology, you name it, we have it.", Max grinned, his blue eyes lighting up. The coughing exploded, breaking the silence in the room. Max's eyes glazed towards the man; his hands folded. "Do you have something to add, Mr. Time?", the short man stood up, his eyes slighted. "Do you really trust this...", The man stuttered, his hands trembled as Max watched eagerly. "This terrorist! He's been selling weapons to your enemies! All this man wants is an arms war, and profit.", Max frowned, beginning to doubt his decisions. "Is this true, Mr. Salem?", Watching closely, he tapped his foot waiting for the tall man's response. "Mr. Burrows, you clearly cannot trust this clown. Do I need to remind you of his last project?", Mr. Salem then turned, facing the short man. "I suggest sticking to bell making.", Mr. Salem quickly sat down, arching his massive shoulders forward, facing him. Max tapped his fingers quietly, pressing down on the glass table with each tap. "Mr. Time, I think we're clearly finished here.", Max spoke, trying to hide the frustration in his voice. "Wait, wait. Mr. Burrows, Can I-I please explain-, Wait!", The short statured man shouted, being carried out of the room by the security forces. Mr. Time jerked hard, stopping inches from Max's face. "One day, this wretched city is going to get it's reckoning, and all your corrupted secrets will be exposed.", Mr. Time spat out, darting out of the room. Face pale as a moon, Max hopped out of the chair heading towards the restroom. His hands fiercely pushed the door open and headed to the golden sink. His heart raced; thoughts scattered into pieces. *"Did he know about the project? No, there's no way he couldn't. Just relax, Max. Breathe."*, Stepping back into the conference room, their eyes settled back on him. "Sorry folks, had to take a breather.", Max smiled, his expression re-assuring the room. "Now, Mr. Salem. About your 'compensation'.", Pausing, he glanced down at the gold watch for a moment before raising his eyes. "Do you happen to have anything related to *experimental* energy tech accessible?", His eyes darted back and forth, hoping to lessen the suspicion. Mr. Salem shifted in his seat, shuffling through the papers. "I do.", Max tapped his foot harder under the table, his excitement rising. "When's the earliest you need?", Mr. Salem asked, raising his thin eyebrows. "Tonight.", He blurted out, his heart began to race again. "That is a tough call Mr. Burrows, but you are my most valuable customer.", The man slid the papers across the glass table, the silver pen rolled towards him. He eagerly picked up the pen, signing diligently. The two men raised from their chairs, shaking hands. Max felt his grip, the uneasy feeling hit his gut. Turning around, he headed out the door, reaching for his phone. Missed calls littered the screen, their notifications accompanied with messages. The phone rang out, vibrating loudly. He raised it to his ear, the voice on the other end blasting his eardrums. "You did what??!", Max held the phone back from his ear, disoriented. "Tom, it was needed. Besides, I think I may have found a solution to our energy consumption issue.", There was a pause on the other end, bringing silence to their conversation. "Tom?", Max asked, beginning to worry. "Sorry, just writing down some calculations.", Max sighed, "I need you to pick the device up by the warehouse and get it to the lab ASAP, understand? I'll be there in about twenty-minutes to see if we can get this running.", He explained, his heart still full of excitement. "Hate to break the news to ya, my man. But..don't you have a date with that bartender from last Friday at five?", Max had completely forgotten, his feet moved quickly, changing his direction towards the restaurant. He hung up, slipping the phone into his pocket and darted towards his late date.

Sophia waited at the table, tapping her foot anxiously. *"Late, should've expected a bit more from the mayor himself."*, Her thoughts poured through her mind, trying to find the reason for her late date. Her brunette hair was curled, her golden skin sparkled under the patio light. She glanced around, her eyes darting towards the entrance. Her late date stumbled inside, combing his hair to the side. Sophia waved at him, grabbing his attention. He smiled back at her; his eyes full of surprise. Max sat down at the table, his tie crooked, his hair wet. "I'm so terribly sorry, I got caught up in some conf-," He stuttered, his hands trembling nervously.

Her rosy perfume was sweet, it overwhelming his nostrils. Grabbing his hand, she laughed at him, trying to lighten the mood. "It's alright. I'm well aware you're a busy man.", She stared into his big blue ocean eyes, feeling his warmth of kindness. "So...how has it been? You're still at the bar down at the east end of town?", Max broke the silence, awkwardly. "Yes, I am. But let's talk about you.", Sophia spoke softly, her aversion subtle. "So, *Mr. Mayor*, tell me a little about yourself. Where are you from?", Her voice was smooth like silk. Max shifted in the chair, finally making eye contact with her. "Well, my parents died when I was around twelve. I've been on my own ever since.", She glanced at his watch, it's golden outline old, but functional. "That watch looks pretty old, family heir?", Her amber eyes watched him nervously glance down at the watch before he spoke again, "Yeah, my father gave it to me before he died. Said a good friend of his gave it to him as a parting gift.", She watched as he glanced down again at his watch before resting his eyes at the menu. "So..what about you? What's your story?", His voice was tight, shaky. Sophia leaned back in the chair, her eyes darting across the room. She tapped her fingers nervously before speaking. "I've been really all over, I came from the southern coast, you know.", Her voice was quiet as she tapped her fingers faster. "Where exactly? If you don't mind me asking.", Max asked, his blue eyes finally gazed into hers. Her foot tapped quickly, her knee bobbled up and down. "North Point.", She blurted out. Sophia smiled faintly. She placed her hands on his hand, lightly tapping his fingers. Her eyes met his. "I thought North Point was destroyed by that nuclear me- ", Coughing violently, he immediately gripped her hands tightly, his eyes full of concern. "Excuse me, I'm just feeling a bit unwell. That's all."

Clearing her throat, she reached to adjust her elegant red dress. "I do have a few questions to ask though, are you really the 'incorruptible' man they speak so highly of? Or are you hiding something, Mr. Burrows?", Sophia grinned, playful tapping her fingers on his hand. She watched his face redden, the shade of tomato red. "I-I Well, you se-.", Her finger pressed against his lips, shushing him. "This was a splendid date, Mr. Burrows. I look forward to our second date. `` Quickly sliding her number, she rose from the chair, waving at the stunned man. Her smile faded outside, the sky was dark, the wind blew hard. Walking down the street, she held tightly to her purse. "I swear the weatherman said clear skies tonight.", Sophia muttered, her hair flying in the wind. "You can't run.", a whispering voice blew through the wind. She swiftly turned, her heart beginning to race. "Hello! Is anyone out there?", Sophia called out, walking faster. Silence was the response to her calling. Her calves burned as she sprinted home, reaching the lit-up porch. "You can't run from your past!", the voice rang out. Swinging the door open, she rushed inside, locking the door behind her. Slowly lowering to the floor, her hot tears rushed down her cheek. Her head against the wall, she slammed it hard. The banging increased; her eyes blurred. With one final bang, the world spun around, slowly dimming. "I'm coming home, my love.", the voice echoed in her head before darkness filled her vision.

Tom sat in the lab; his eyes glued to the computer screen in front of him. Bags of chips littered the desk, the crumbs in the creases of the keys. Tom leaned back, his arm slamming on the small black button, unaware of his triggering. Red lights flashed silently on the walls as Tom stared at the computer screen, oblivious. Machinery whirred alive; the faint echoes of screams whispered throughout the containment room. Dim lights bounced off the steel door as it creaked. Creaking loudly, the containment door held on as the wind blew harder. Tom's eyes quickly glanced around the room, shrugging. Glass shifted, the pressure rising. The steel hinges creaked louder as his eye darted between the screen and the room. Shrugging again, the chips crunching loudly in the bag. Screams echoed louder throughout the containment room, the lights shining brighter. Machinery shifted and creaked, masked by the noise of a rustling bag. The door let out a loud shifting noise, the bag of chips dropped onto the desktop. Footsteps shuffled lazily towards the containment window, as gasping was heard from the man. The steel hinges bent, as the door swung open. Rushing in, it's a cold, crisp feeling that touches the man's face. Papers darted across the room, the chair rolling towards the containment room. His hair blew violently, his eyes wild with excitement. Making his trek across the room, the phone laid on the desk, untouched. Dialing, it rang out loudly as he held onto the desk. Steel snapped in half, the door flying towards the epicenter. The line rang out one final time before ceasing, his face now full of fear. Papers flung towards the containment room, the glass shattering into millions of pieces, Feet sliding, his hands clamped on the wooden desk. It shook, the legs shifted as the wind blew harder. His hands were a deep red, holding on to the buckling desk, fingers slowly edged, his grip tight. The front legs lifted up as Tom held on tighter. Chip bags flew past him, being sucked into the vortex. Sliding off the table, it flung itself into the air, missing Tom's head by inches. The wooden leg lightly grazed his messy hair, the structure ripped apart before his eyes. Nails deep into the concrete floor, grunting and scratching were his only options. His skin rubbed against the ragged concrete; his bloody fingernails held on to the floor with immense effort. The screams raged louder, mixing in with the howling wind that deafened Tom's ears. Hands now bloody, a shade of blue, he slid towards the containment room, clawing at the floor. The alarm's red lights shone brightly, its siren blasting loudly into his ears. The phone flew past Tom, lighting up as it rang out. His hands cut deep into the broken hinges, his eyes expressing desperation. Droplets of blood stained his face, his fingers beginning to slip. Letting out a scream, he felt his body fly through the room, lights whirred across his vision. Darkness followed suit, his body crashing into the cold dirt. The air was still, the silence almost unnatural. Tom shifted, raising his hand to his head. The dead forest around him stood still, as he groaned. His jeans ripped and his hands blood stained, Tom slowly rose from the ground. The sky was darker than night, no moon glistened, it's an eerie glow here. His vision spun; the grey ambience of the portal caught his eyes. The cold dirt met his face, as Tom tumbled back to the ground, his body ached. Swift footsteps broke the veil of silence provoking fear into Tom's face. The cold sweat broke out across his face as he began to crawl towards the portal. Objects littered the ground beside him, the footsteps increasing in volume. Tom crawled faster, groaning in agony. The cold whispers of breathing closed in on his left. A tense body, sweat poured down his face, frozen. Slithering, the creature finally entered his field of view. The tentacles slowly slid across his arms; his arms shivered at the feeling. It stood tall looking off at the shining portal. Tom's muscles stiffened further; his eyes glued to the creature. His shirt soaked with sweat; he didn't dare to move any muscle. Flesh tendrils morphed, twisting into bones, shoulders formed. It's face softened, eye sockets becoming clear. Tom watched, his eyes full of disgust, but an insatiable curiosity kept him glued to the figure in front of him. The man stood in front of the portal smiling; his emerald eyes full of joy. "I'm finally home.", his voice cracked, the flash of grey light erupted before leaving Tom in the eerie darkness.

Max opened his eyes, feeling the dusty wind blow across his face. His head laid against the hot sand, feeling the particles rub against his cheeks. Rising from the dirt, he gazed across the desolate wasteland. Buildings after buildings, obliterated. Shards of glass littered the ground and ash covered the streets in abundance. The overwhelming stench masked the air, his stomach churned in response. The mighty town hall once stood luxurious and a symbol of power, now nothing but ashes in the wind. Skulls were scattered around it, flesh rotting. Like a massive mountain, they were stacked high. He stared up at the makeshift throne, empty. It's structure was grotesque, flesh-like. His heart began to race, *"No. No, no. This couldn't be the work of that portal. Father's work explained it as a paradise."*, Max climbed up the mountain of skulls, reaching the top quickly. Examining the throne, his stomach twisted at the sight of it. "I suppose that one day you could fulfill my role. My destiny.", A voice spoke loudly, coming from the bottom of the mountain. Max watched the man slowly step over the skulls with ease, his grey business suit was polished, his fedora was tipped, concealing his eyes. "I was once a god, ruling over cities with ease, before your kind locked me away in hell. Imprisoned for decades, now free.", Max stepped back, stumbling down the hill. The man laughed; his impossible smile widened. Max felt a hand on his arm, it's cold ethereal touch clawed at his skin. He crawled backwards, watching the corpse stumble out of the pile of skulls. "Max..", its voice croaked. "Dad?", Max questioned the corpse, watching with a hint of curiosity. "I warned you, brea-", His father's corpse fell limp, its eyes rolling back. "What?", Max's eyes watered up, feeling anger rise to his throat. "Ah, family. I used to have a family.", The man chuckled. Max felt the bottled-up anger spring into action, "What do you want from me?!", Max screamed, his fists clenched. "To corrupt even the purest of souls. The storm is coming, Mr. Burrows. Prepare.", His voice whispered into Max's ear, taunting him. The siren wailed, waking Max from his dream. His eyes darted across the room, the dread overwhelming his senses. Max quickly grabbed his shoes, running out of the bedroom door. He reached for the phone on the dark wooden table, reading the notifications. *"Three missed calls..."*, His fingers pressed down on the screen, the line ringing. *"Voicemail again."*, Max slammed the phone down on the table, grabbing the remote.

"As you can see here, what appears to be an earthquake has hit Silent Falls violently. Locals reported seeing floating figures in the sky, more information will be released as soon a-", The news broadcast explained, before being cut off. He felt the immense dread hit his stomach; his feet ran out of the door. Max ran through the rain as people quietly walked through the streets with umbrellas in hand, the look on their faces, distraught and worried. Max turned down the street and noticed that the buildings looked worse here, the trees from the park torn apart, the leaves scattered, the post office, torn into pieces as mail soaked into the mud. Then, he found the hole. Massive in size, it covered most of where Central Park was. Confused by the more severe destruction, it clicked in his mind. *"The lab, something went off in the lab."*, Max thought, his eyes wide with fear. Max hurried down the mud-like hole and slid, scraping his knee on the rocks. Then he saw the faint light of the lamp in his office. Jumping down and moving a few of the smaller rocks, he fell down into the distraught and broken lab. The computer lay on its side and the monitor cracked but was functional. The blue screen and the dark red font seem to indicate something went wrong with the portal. The containment door lay open, the portal still active. A paper was laid on the floor and read, "You've been doomed from the start, now it's time for reckoning.", Max first confused at the odd note, remembered his dream from the night before. *"It had to be connected, but where is Tom?"*, his thoughts were scattered at the destruction around him. The portal shone brightly, emitting its static noise. Max knew one thing, if the dream was coming true, he had to get everyone out. The sound of the rain poured harder into the hole prompting him to leave before it became too hard to navigate through the weather. Max stopped and turned and looked at the activated portal. *"If this is causing the chaos, why am I just standing here about to leave this thing activated?"*, Max scanned the room for a hammer. Under the rubble laid a sledgehammer they had reserved for emergencies. He walked inside the containment room and began to hit the portal frame, it cracked with ease and the light flickered. Max slammed the portal again, and heard the voice of a thousand people screaming in terror. The sounds of souls trapped in a dark dimension with no escape. **BANG**, Max hit the portal again, prompting its chilling noise of terror and fear. The portal cracked and fell apart, turning into dust. He felt lightheaded, and dizzy. But all his mind told him was, "*GET OUT OF HERE.*", Max darted out of the hole, climbing out of the mud. Lightning struck wildly across the gray sky, the rain poured hard and the wind blew in every direction. His dress pants were covered with wet mud, staining them for a lifetime. Max's hair blew wildly in the wind. The sense of dread and doom loomed over his head, knowing this wasn't going to end well. Glancing around, umbrellas raised up clustered together. The emergency broadcast system blared loudly notifying the citizens to exit the city border. Its eerie wail made the disoriented mayor shiver in cold sweat. Stumbling forward, Max headed towards the border, head down as he dragged his muddy dress shoes down the street. The sky continued its raging storm, droplets of rain pouring down like a barrage of bullets. The cryptic message rang out in his head loudly, he tried to make sense of it. *"Is this really my fault?"*, his thoughts echoed quietly as he continued through the streets, rubble scattered in large pieces. The ground rumbled below, sounds of buildings shifted and groaned in the distance. Max neared the border, taken aback by the damage down to the city walls. Metal twisted; the checking point obliterated into ashes. Bodies lay across the again, limbs torn off and scattered. Max tried to avoid looking at their disassembled forms, his stomach churned, making the man gag violently. Quickly stepping past the bodies, Max briskly walked towards the clearing in the distance where the crowd of his people stood. The sky darkened to an eerie shade of red, causing him to briefly stop and examine the phenomenon. He looked back at the crowd of people, and sighed. "I think I'll blame this mistake in the weather, quite literally.", Max mumbled to himself and began approaching them, his eyes scanning the crowd for Sophia, hoping she got out in time. The images of the bodies ingrained in his mind as he winced at the idea that his beloved could've been one of the mangled bodies.

Sophia darted through the incoming crowds, trying to search for Max. She knew she couldn't keep going backwards towards the city, an evacuation order was in place and she didn't want to be there when whatever was going on got worse. The wind howled and blew its cold rain over the crowd that neared the border. The sky seemed to change from the oblivion of black to a dark green shade which shifted as the thunder began to roll above, the dark lightning an eerie purple as the wind raged stronger. Max appeared through the crowd as it dispersed and parted a way for their leader to pass. His face darkened by a look of fear, which she had never seen before. A thousand questions arose from the crowd, "Where are we supposed to go?", a man yelled out, "Yeah, what is even going on?", another woman yelled, the fear in their voices. "Alright, calm down everyone.", Max spoke in a reassuring tone hiding his fear from the crowd. "We are going to head to Cecilia, our *wonderful* neighbor who offered refuge in their city for the time being.", Max continued. The murmurs from the crowd, shocked and in fear. "Alright, let's get moving!", Max yelled as the crowd moved past the checking point and into the wilderness. In the distance, the infantry of Cecillia moved closer to the city, causing discomfort across the crowd. The captain stopped and spoke with concern, his northern accent thick and hard to understand, "Heard ya got something wild in there, ain't nothin' to us boys." Max shook his head; he knew this wasn't going to end well. "Just get in there, get the job done and don't wreck what's left of my city, Cecillian.", The captain smiled and motioned his men to go. He whispered, "Heard you got a really nice jewelry store in there, hope ya don't mind me shopping a little.", Max shook his head and waved at the city's inhabitants to move towards the lake which lay a mile ahead in the dark fog.

The captain turned to his squadron, motioning them to enter the city. With his 4 men at his side, guns at the sky and ground, they searched for the invisible threat. Bodies laid next to the torn walls, blood stained on their clothes and the street. "Boss! Looks like an animal came through here and shredded these poor officers to pieces. Never hadn't a chance.", One of the soldiers commented, bending down and observing their wounds. "You scared of a bear, Goose?", Another soldier chimed in, taunting him. The soldier named Goose peered closer at one of the bodies, examining the massive claw marks. He looked up at the rest of the squadron. "Whatever it was, it sure wasn't no bear.", The other soldiers laughed, "What if it was one of those, you know, big clawed beasts from that legend! Legend says, Emperor Connor defeated one single handedly.", The captain shook his head, examining the damage of the walls. "That old man couldn't even beat a fox if it was tied up- ", The captain stepped forward to the soldiers, grabbing one by the throat. His hand clenched tightly as the soldier's face began to turn a shade of purple. "You will not disrespect our leader! You will not doubt your loyalty! "The captain slammed the soldier against a pillar of stone, holding them in a chokehold. The soldier's face turned a deep purple as he tried to breathe. "Do you understand me?", The captain screamed at him, his voice full of anger. The soldier lifted his thumb up as a sign of agreement. Letting go, the captain turned to the rest of the squadron, "Keep moving, we have plenty more to cover!" Silence fell across the city as the rain lifted, leaving only the wind and the dark clouds in the evening sky. As they closed in on the park, the massive sinkhole covered a small portion of the park. Motioning the soldiers, they slid down the sinkhole, rocks tumbling at their sides. The lab's entrance was torn apart, papers laid on the ground, stomped and covered with mud. The computer displayed a large red text, 'CONTAINMENT FAILURE IMMINENT. EVACUATE IMMEDIATELY.' "What in tarnation were these imbeciles up to?", Captain said aloud, examining the papers on the desk. He approached the containment door, the sirens silently flashing their red warnings. The titanium hinges were twisted and bent; the door handle laid on the ground. Stepping inside, the captain readied his gun, preparing to meet the source of the destruction. His palms were sweaty, his eyes darted back and forth, everything was in silence. Only the wind from outside could be heard. He glanced around only to find his eyes on a middle-aged man in the corner, cigarette in hand, lit. The captain instinctively pointed his weapon at the mysterious man, his finger on the trigger. "Come on out, hands up.", The captain spoke, his voice raspy but trying to sound in control. The mysterious man stepped forward, tossing the cigarette on the ground carelessly. "You people amuse me. Truly, you amuse me with your toys, your 'politics', your *pointless lives.*", The man adjusted his fedora, stepping closer to the armed captain. "Mankind was supposed to be extraordinary, kings and queens of the universe around us. But now, all you do is play your petty games and worry how you'll pay next month's bills. Speaking of bills, I haven't paid mine in, let's see here." The man glanced down at his golden watch. "About twenty-three years to be exact.", The captain pointed the gun at the man, irritated. "You have thirty seconds to comply or be shot.", his voice full of tension. The man continued talking carelessly, "All these rules, *order.* I can truly show you a raw power young man. All the answers you've been seeking, can be accessed. Anyways, what's up with these 'comply or be shot these days, I remember back before I got trapped in hell, they just shot ya dead. Too much paperw-,″ Bullets pierced the man's chest, causing blood to spill out as he collapsed onto the ground. The captain stood, finger still on the trigger. The other soldiers were behind him, watching in horror. "Clear out gentlemen. We still gotta find the source of the incident.", The group began to head back towards the entrance of the sinkhole when a voice spoke up from the back of the room. "You know, flesh is only a temporary form in the eventual ascension of humanity. I can offer you a path to true power, true ascension." Turning around, the captain's expression was full of confusion. The man's hands were a shade of the night sky, his emerald eyes glowed brightly. The captain stood still, his hands clammy and tight. The cold sweat beaded across his forehead. Yet again, his fingers were on the trigger of his rifle. "Fire.", His voice came out, raspy and hushed. The sounds of bullets exploded across the room, tearing into flesh. The man still stood there, bullet holes in his suit. The captain's face turned stone cold; his arms twitched slightly. Behind the captain, the sound of footsteps retreating echoed across the room as one of the soldiers began to run towards the entrance. A heavy thump hit the ground, the soldiers turned to see their fellow member sliced into pieces, blood spraying on to the walls. "Focus fire!", Hot barrels erupted like a volcano, a voice ringing over the gunfire. Shreds of clothing fabric rained down across the shattered laboratory, the droplets of rain quietly poured down, silence rushing in a breeze of the cold wind. Blood and iron overwhelmed his senses, his body frozen. "Enjoy the rest of the show.", the mystery man spoke, his voice shattering like glass. Piercing his chest, the shard of metal ruptured the man's heart, leaving blood to spray wildly across the bloody room. His knees buckled, gravity pulled down on the captain, his confused eyes could only raise up to look at the god-like being before collapsing onto the cold muddy concrete floor. Roses fell around him, their sweet scent radiating into his nostrils. Footsteps quickly left his dying body, leaving only the rain to be his final sound. The man closed his eyes, breathing in the sweet scent of the roses one final time. His last breath, letting out a final sigh as his body laid limp on the laboratory floor.

The sky was an eerie red, the storm raged on, the wind blowing hard like daggers of air. Max walked through the scared crowd, their faces worrisome and confused. He smiled, faking, trying to assure them with a false sense of security. Standing in the middle, the cold sweat poured down his face, his heart began to race. *"I can't tell them I did this. No way."*, His thoughts echoed. Clearing his throat, he spoke, his voice cracking. "My people, this is simply a severe weather event occurring, I assure you everything is under control.", He felt their anger, their fear builds up. "Under control? Does this seem like under control to you! Huh?", A tall, slender man called out. Followed by shouts of agreement, he tensed up. "Calm down, I promise everything is handled. We have external forces investigating the city for damage.", The crowd whispered among themselves, as a short, plump woman stepped forward, her tattered clothes ripped. "Look at you. You have no idea what's going on! You let those terrorists in our city! They're probably looting my house right now.", Max paused, breathing in, his anger rising. "Now, there is no reason to insult our friends here. They offered to help, I accepted." His tone was firm, his eyes blazing, anger was at the tip of his tongue. "Look! In the sky!", A man called out, pointing at the levitating figure descending over the crowd. Max's eyes squinted, watching the dark figure float over the townspeople. His heart sank, the figure descending into the field. The crowd parted; their eyes locked onto the mysterious man. "Hello, Max.", his familiar voice echoed, the man's emerald eyes shone brightly. His knees began to buckle, but he tried to stand tall and solid. "You people seem to doubt your leaders, your *rulers*.", The man spoke, his voice clear and stern. "Do you trust this man to lead you? This failure?", The crowd murmured, voices whispered in agreement, their eyes turned to each other, looking for clarity. "What if I told you, this man was the cause of the events that unfolded today."The man continued, smiling as the crowd gasped in response to his revelation. Max's heart sank deeper, his hands clenched tight. "I don't hear no denying, Mr. Burrows.", The man spoke again, chuckling. "Well, it seems you cannot trust your leaders to lead. I've come to change that.". A short man with a grey suit stepped out of the crowd, his gold watch shimmered in the dim light. "Why should we trust you? You could be just like the others.", The mysterious man shrugged his shoulders, laughing. "Let me introduce myself, I am Stardust, an ancient god watching over humanity. I've come to prevent your own destruction from this man, Mr. Burrows here.", He pointed at Max, his eyes locked onto him. Max let go, his eyes blazed with blinded rage. He charged towards the god-like being, screaming wildly. Stardust turned, chuckling. He raised his hand, hurtling Max to the ground. "Let the battle commence.", Stardust quietly spoke, fog quickly settled in, leaving only Max in his view. Max groaned loudly, gripping the mud. Hands covered in mud, he rushed towards Stardust, only to be slammed back to the ground. "Mr. Burrows, your efforts are...futile. You are destined to lose this battle."

"I will not let this city be ruled by you!", Max stood up, his hands tainted with blood. "Who said it would be ruled by me?", Stardust laughed, looking at the weak man. "My powers may be decreased, but I will not allow you to foil my plans.", Max felt the wind blow harder, his feet slid in the mud. He turned to see the portal appear out of thin air. Stardust grabbed Max's tie, dragging the man towards the portal. Max screamed for help, his voice tight, gasping for air. "Sophia!", He called out, struggling to breathe. "No one can hear you, Max. Ever been skydiving?", The god asked, his tone sarcastic. "Wha- ", Max was quickly cut off, thrown into free fall. His vision whirled around him; the thin air sliced under his arms. The ground was hard, dryer than a desert. Max groaned in pain, his vision settling around him. "Glad I'm not the only person banished to hell here.", A voice shouted, the familiarity of the voice coming to him. He shifted forward, the figure coming in clarity. "Yeah, the fall hurt for a few hours. You'll be healed soon enough.", Tom reached his hand out, pulling Max up off the ground. "I- I thought you were a dead man.", Max stammered, his arms reaching around the man tightly. "I suppose you could've answered your phone a bit earlier.", Tom chucked, trying to make light of the dark situation. Max took in the sight, the starless night. The barren plains were a pale green, the dim light seemed to have no visible source. "So…what exactly do we know?", Max asked, clinging to a hope in his head. Tom sighed, shaking his head slightly. "Well to tell you the truth, I'm clueless." The slow realization settled in, the hard truth slicing at Max's heart. "Today, we'll set up camp, tomorrow, we'll search for answers." Max said weakly, his voice cracking at the thought of his city being destroyed. "Forgive me, my love.", Max whispered in the starless sky.

Stardust watched the portal close, smiling. "*I suppose I can't fool these idiots with this form.*", His skin split open, forming a tan shade, his head morphed. His suit became a tattered shirt, mud slung over it. He spoke, clearing his throat. "Hello, I'm Max Burrows, your mayor.", His voice morphed, lowering in pitch with an accent. "*Fools. Won't even tell the difference.*" With a swipe of his hand, the fog began to lift. The crowd was still gathered around, their faces full of curiosity. They began to cheer, their faces lifting up. "Do you doubt me now as your leader?", He called out, and the crowd roared loudly. "Now! My people! Let us reclaim our city!", Stardust shouted, the crowd rushing towards their wrecked city. He watched as the crowd dispersed, wiping the mud off his black dress pants. "Max! Thank goodness you're safe!", A brunette rushed towards him, wrapping her arms around him. "*This must be Sophia.*", He thought, grabbing her tightly. "I'm alright, darling. We won't ever have to worry about that demon again.", Sophia slowly pulling away, looking into his eyes. "My love, I thought about what you said at our date last night, I think I truly love you; I just feel this undeniable connection around you.", His tone was smooth, his influence affecting her. "I-I, wow Max, that's sudden.

But I think. I-I,", Sophia stuttered, her rosy cheeks hot. "It's alright. I know it's sudden.", He spoke, his voice soothing. "I-I love you too, Max Burrows.", She reached up, kissing his lips passionately. He leaned back, breaking the kiss. The rain lightened up, the clouds slowly breaking away, revealing the evening sunlight. Stardust grabbed her hand, walking back towards their city.

His purple robe gently dragged across the marble floor of the palace, his sandals flopping loudly. Emperor Marcus frowned, his eyes gazing down at the dead soldiers before him. "Do you know who did this?", Marcus asked, his voice was quiet, his anger at the tip of his tongue. "My lord, these are the bodies that we recovered from the lab. Seems like they were butchered by some large animal.", the servant spoke, his voice quivering. "You mean to tell me? That my best warriors got cut up by some animal in a lab?", Marcus shouted, his eyes blazed with anger. "My lord, I-I, It seems that would be a probable cause.", the servant cowered down to the floor, flinching. "No..these marks aren't primal. These.", Marcus stopped mid-sentence, freezing. His hands were clammy, his face felt pale. "Dispose of these bodies immediately, if I dare see one of ye speak of this incident, I'll shred ya myself.", His voice tightened, his eyes flared at the soldiers. Rushing up the stairs, Marcus slammed the door shut. He sat down at the light brown desk, holding his hand to his head. Pulling his robe back, the scar on his side was old, but still visible. *"It couldn't be, I killed the beast centuries ago!"*, Marcus thought, his mind scattering to a thousand re-assuring conclusions. Sliding the drawer open, the small blade shimmered brightly against the brown desk. He raised it up, the reflection of his blade revealed a grey-haired man, his fedora dipped down, the grey tie was neatly placed. Marcus dropped the blade, jumping back. It hit the ground, ringing out. "You will not terrorize me in my own home, demon!", Marcus shouted, quickly throwing the blade into the wall. "My lord, are you alright?", The servant called out, knocking on the door. The door swung open, the servant gasping for air. "I told you to never disturb me in my royal room!", Marcus bellowed, his hand tightening around his neck. He swung the man against the wall, groaning quietly, he quickly scattered down the stairs bleeding wildly. Marcus slammed the door shut and reached for the phone on the dresser.

"How soon can you have the rocket prepped?"

"Five to six months minimum, my lord."

"We don't have that kind of time."

"I suppose I can push it to four, my lord."

Marcus slammed the phone on the ground, the pieces shattering like glass. His rage erupted, his hands barraging the brick walls until they bled. With a final blow, Marcus collapsed to the ground, silently weeping. He raised his head looking out the window at the night sky. A single star shone brightly, reminding him of his destiny. Marcus wiped the tears off his face, smearing the blood onto his cheeks. Rising from the floor, he opened the door, his bare chest showing his massive scars. Descending the stairs, his soldiers stood in formation, their eyes watched the walls. Not one of them dared to question the bloody man, their faces remained solid. The massive palace doors swung open; the dim moonlight peaked through the clouds. "Matthias! Get me my horse.", Marcus called out to the young soldier. The young man rushed back quickly, guiding the black horse towards his ruler. Mounting the saddle, the emperor took off reaching Cecillia's limits in minutes. The wind blew through his short hair, his eyes gazing across the vast, cold plains. An hour had passed before he'd seen the dim lights of Octavia, a small city that broke off from Cecillia's vast northern empire recently. The massive cobblestone wall stood towering. Below, the entrance was guarded by armed guards, alert. Marcus approached the entrance hopping off the horse, holding his hands up. "I need to speak to Prime Minister Davis, it's urgent.", The guards pointed their weapons at him, tense and hostile. "Why should we believe you? Cecilian scum!", One of the guards spat, stepping closer. "I assure you, my intentions are pure.", He explained, the guards stepping closer. His hands slid behind his back, grasping for the dagger in his back pocket. They stepped closer, their guns pointed at his chest. "Suppose I'll have to do this the hard way, eh?", Marcus muttered, the dagger in his hand. "Hello, old friend.", A voice broke through the tense silence, walking into the streetlight. "I see you've really cracked down on security, ya?", Marcus asked, his northern accent strong. "Well, I've learned from my past mistakes, speaking after your invasion attempts failed.", The man's voice was bitter, his hatred was clear. "But, to come down here yourself? Did you finally decide to get off your lazy bottom and face me on my own turf?", Dwaine continued, spitting at the man in disgust. "It's about *Him*.", Marcus quickly spoke, his tone was cold. He watched Dwaine turn, his face ran cold. "Why didn't you say so? Please come in!", Dwaine said, his voice cheery. Inside the walls, the small town was rustic, the gravel roads were widespread. The two men entered the brick town hall, heading towards the small office in the back. The dim lights illuminated the walls, paintings hung all over the room. Dwaine motioned him to sit down in the wooden chair. "Are you sure it was him?", Dwaine's voice was tight, his eyes darted back and forth. Marcus leaned forward, locking his eyes onto Dwaine. "Yes. The storm was a sign. My men were sliced into pieces!", Marcus raised his voice. "We should've destroyed that city when we had the chance.", He continued. "No, we must warn Max. We cannot make the same mistake as before.", Dwaine paced around the room, his hands trembling. "Warn him? It is far too late for that, my friend. The cage has been opened. Max will die with his people!", Marcus rose from the chair, his voice raised. He looked down at the smaller man, his face full of anger. "It is far too late for all of us." Quickly exiting the room, he left the dark building. The night sky shimmered with stars, the cold wind breezed across his face. He smiled, looking up at the bright star that illuminated the starry night. "Soon.", Marcus whispered in the wind. "Soon..",

James stared at the paperwork laid on his desk. He felt the tiny wrinkles in his forehead, his fingers tried to push them back. Leaning back in his chair, his eyes stared up at the massive paintings on the grey walls. The paintings depicted gods, immortal beings of strength and glory. He often found himself daydreaming, his body immortal, like a high god. The phone rang, his senses rushing back to his desk. James sighed loudly, grunting to reach the phone. "I told you Mary, do not let that whore call me aga-,", His voice was irritable, "Sir, it's the mayor.", The receptionist cut him off sharply. James sat up in the chair, his eyes displayed a sense of curiosity. "Send him up immediately.", The call was swiftly ended with a slamming of the phone. Moments later, the elevator chimed allowing Stardust to enter the wide office. James stood up, fixing his tie. He smiled, reaching his hand out to the man. Stardust quickly obliged; his grip tight. The two men sat down, their faces blank. "What offer do you have now to sell me, Mr. Burrows?", James asked, his tone professional, his eyes settling on the man's gray tie. "I'm afraid, this simply cannot be bought. Only obtained.", Stardust explained, his emerald eyes were sharp. "Mr. Burrows, I'm not getting the memento here.", James tapped his fingers along the rich mahogany desk. "I can offer you, Immortality.", Stardust raised his hands, his voice was majestic. James tried to keep himself from bursting out of laughter, but he couldn't. "You..really are crazy aren't you, Mr. Burrows.", He continued, his face red. Stardust only sat there, his face was solid, his eyes were serious. "Man, I can't believe you'd try to fo-", James's tie was quickly pulled, his laughter turned to gasps for air. Stardust pulled harder; his face only remained grim. James tried to swing at the man to get him to let go. Darkness shrouded him; his vision was blocked. The heat seared at his skin, leaving burn marks. Grasping at his throat, James still tried to breathe. Then, the smoke cleared. His head hit the ground, the tie loosened. His throat opened back up, letting in the cold air of the laboratory. James struggled to get up off the floor. His deep breathing was loud, his vision began to clear. Standing over him, Stardust looked down at him, smiling. "Welcome, Mr. Salem.", Stardust laughed, reaching his hand out to James. "H-how did we get here?", James swung his head around, trying to make sense of it all. "I understand you may have a lot of questions.", Stardust stated, walking towards the containment room. "Power, it's a beautiful thing. It changes you. It *transforms* you.", The man continued on, looking through the glass at the halfway-built portal. "When I first came to Silent Falls, I saw your name plastered on billboards, everywhere. I saw a man with power. A man who wanted more power.", Stardust turned to face James, his eyes wild with excitement. . "I can offer you that! I can offer you unlimited power. I can offer you god-like powers.", James frowned, waiting to hear the bad part. "What's the catch, where's the price? My soul, my life?", His voice echoed across the room, questions barreling out. "All I ask is your support. The rebuilding of the portal has taken far too long alone. It is the key to everything. Then we will reap the rewards, the gateway will be opened and Silent Falls will no longer be a slave to the Northern countries." His hands sat at his side, trying to process it all. "Hold on, what did you mean when you first came to Silent Falls? You're the mayor, you founded this city." His questions made Stardust uneasy. He watched the man step forward, shaking his head. "Well, the key to living oblivious to the corruption around you, is to simply reassure yourself. Don't let your mind ask questions. Questions make you aware."

Stardust's hands shaked, his body shuddered. His skin morphed, twisted into a pale tone. James watched in horror, backing towards the wall. "You're that demon! The one that Max defeated six months ago! Ho- ", The questions rushed off his tongue, before being cut off by the man. "Mr. Salem, I can assure you, Mr. Burrows is somewhere *safe.* I couldn't let him get in the way of the plans I have.", James reached for the holster grasping for the pistol on his hip. "You know, bullet holes in my nice suit are getting old.", Stardust laughed, stepping closer to James. His eyes darted to Stardust's hands, where his gun was held. Stardust squeezed the trigger. The shot fired off hitting the wall beside him. James cowered down, flinching at the sound of the bullet whizzing past his head. "Surely we can work out a deal! I have plenty of money!", James quietly spoke, his hands held in front of his head. Stardust waved the gun around, "I don't want your money, Mr. Salem. I want your *support*. I'm offering you a chance to become a god like myself! Yet, you cower to the sound of a bullet!", Stardust shouted, throwing the gun across the room. James slowly rose up, looking down at his captor. "I-I understand.", He stammered. "Very well. But I need one final thing from you.", James watched as the man stepped closer, raising his hand. "Your *undying* loyalty.", James felt the man's hand press on his chest. The heat seared at his skin. He screamed in agony, collapsing to the floor. "Let it consume you, only then will you find the power you've been searching for.", The words echoed in his mind. The searing pain roared harder; his eyes struggled to stay open. Slamming his eyes shut, the heat burned at his eyes. The waves of consciousness slipped away, knocking him out. Moments later, James flung his hands up in defense, looking around the office. He sighed loudly. Raising his shirt, his body was untouched. No signs of burns were present whatsoever. Leaning back in the chair in relief, the sticky note stuck to the side of the desk. He examined it before picking up the phone.

"I'm in."

"Wonderful, but we need more."

"Who else could we trust?"

"Call Mr. Time, he seems to be running out of luck these days."

"Gladly, Mr. *Burrows*.",

The call ended abruptly. James smiled at the paintings, admiring the god-like figures. "Soon, we'll be gods. Soon."

The bells rang loudly as Sophia approached the front of the church, the luxurious red carpet brushing against the bottom of her red wedding dress. Max smiled, watching the beauty, knowing that this day would come. She walked closer and stared at his blue ocean eyes, admiring him. "Do you, Max Burrows, take Sophia as your lovely wife, and do you swear to defend her until the day you die?", the priest asked, proposing the vows. "I do,", Max said, smiling ear to ear. "Sophia, do you take this man as your husband and swear to support him through his journey?", the priest asked Sophia. "I-I, No, there's someone else I love.", Sophia stuttered, the crowd gasping. The church door swung open, as a man wearing a fine gray suit and a fedora walked in. Sophia smiled at Stardust, "I take him as my husband!", the crowd in shock at her statement. Max felt the rage boil inside of him, his face turning blood red. Stardust smiled, as Sophia approached him and said, "I do, I take this man in marriage, not the fool on that stage!", Max clenched his fists, and tried to charge at Stardust. He ran but was stopped dead still by Stardust who simply held his arm out and smiled maliciously. "The time for heroes is gone, Max. It's time you *wake up*.", Max awoke abruptly, hitting his head on the roof of the small wooden shelter. The spot where Tom's bedding lay was empty prompting him to exit the shelter and walk outside. Max glanced at the starless-sky and sighed. Tom carried a basket which held strange fruit. One of the few edible sources of food. "Another nightmare?", Tom asked, looking at Max's raged state and clenched fists. "Yeah, they're getting married." Max sighed and sat against the large tree, feeling defeated. "I suppose that's a little better than watching her die.", Tom, his blunt tone, refusing to hide the dire consequences of the situation. "She doesn't even know it's him, she lives with it every day and she doesn't even know the truth.", Max said, his voice echoing off the shelter. "Max, I think she'll figure out one day and I'm sure it's best she didn't know, for her own safety.", Tom explained, trying to cheer up the guy. Max sighed at the response, hoping for a positive reassurance to this dark dimension. Tom sat the basket down, glancing up at the sky. "I miss the stars; I do miss the birds. "Hey, at least it's better than those pelicans that stole our hotdogs that one summer.", Tom laughed, remembering the days of joy they once had. Max walked into the shelter and grabbed a remote. He stepped outside and pointed it at the large tree. The sounds of the dish on the top of the tree groaned loudly, and began to vibrate the ground. The dish adjusted itself and Max pressed another button. The sound of the laser and its intensity powered up, quickly drowning the area with its sounds. "Do you think it'll work!", Tom yelled at Max trying to talk over the machinery. The laser shone brightly in the dark sky, lighting up the area. Directly in front of Max a portal slowly appeared, it's grey hue like a dark cloud. Max yelled in excitement, "It's working! It's working!!" Tom hurried past the machinery preparing his things. "If this works, we could be free. Free from the torture of solitude, and this hellscape.",The man thought, his mind full of opportunities and ideas. Bag in hand, Tom exited the small shack and headed towards the opening portal. The wind blew hard around the two men, their overgrown hair waving ever so slightly. Max stepped forward, hands trembling. Tom nodded at him in confirmation. Stepping into the portal, the flashing lights blinding him as a wave of heat blistered his skin. Then, the light settled. He couldn't handle what he saw, his eyes watered up, tears swelling. Falling to his knees, the dust scattered across him. The sounds of a roaring wind echoed loudly in the distance. Tom exited the portal, it's ominous noises still in the background. All

Max could feel was defeat. The massive pyramid stood tall, its sandy steps stained red with blood in the distance. A thousand skulls littered the area around the two, the flesh eaten away from decay and age. "What is this place? Where's Silent...Falls...", Tom spoke, his voice full of confusion and sorrow, realizing the truth. Max turned back and looked up at the older man, "He did it.", The pain was unbearable for Max, Stardust had succeeded entirely. A paper flew in the wind as Tom snatched it to examine it. It's burnt edges and poked holes made it hard to read but still legible. "New ruler established, Max Burrows missing for 22 years...", Tom muttered, reading off the article. "Max look!" Tom pointed at the date of the publication. "April 18th, 2045..." Facing Tom, Max stared at him with cold, dark eyes, his face solemn. "We've been gone for 22 years, Tom!", He swing his hands wildly to express his frustration and confusion, "We have to find Sophia. We have to find the rest of the city, surely they hid somewhere in sola-," Tom interrupted wildly, grabbing Max by the shoulders, pulling him in. "Max. There is no one left! Sophia is dead.", The dread in his voice tried to plead with the man. But in his mind, he knew the man wouldn't listen. "She's not dead! I know!", Max yelled out, his arms waving, "Max.", Tom paused, trying to convince him otherwise. "She's gone, man.", Max let out his rage, "No! She's alive!", He screamed wildly, shoving Tom to the ground and began to punch him fiercely. His blood boiled like a fire, and his fists were the steam of his rage. Tom's nose bled an eerie black substance, running down his cheek as Max continued to punch the man. "Max..", Tom gasped, trying to speak to his captor. Max raised his dark, bloody fists and looked at them. *"Why does it feel so good, to pour the rage on another man."* Max thought, realizing that he'd been corrupted all this time. "I... Tom.", Pausing, he let out a sigh, letting the slow realization of what he did. The beaten man laid there, his head fuzzy and face smeared with his dark blood. He slowly groaned, rising up slowly to meet Max face to face. "It's time to go back Max, there is no place here for us. We'll find another way back.", The man winced in pain, his voice rising higher as he scooted up, preparing to get up in the least painful way he could. The rage was silent inside Tom, he felt it deep, but it would only corrupt him further if he gave in to his violent desires. Giving up and giving in would only further things in the direction of his pronounced nemesis, and everything in his right mind told him that Silent Falls couldn't afford that, reality itself couldn't. The two men hobbled and walked towards the open portal, knowing they may never come back to what was left of their home. As Max stepped forward into the portal, the sounds of a familiar voice echoed across the wasteland, making him stop in his tracks. "Sophia?", Max questioned, turning his head and scanning the desolate desert for any sign of her. "What are you doi-", Tom was quickly interrupted as Max darted past him, running across the ruins. "Hey! Where are you going?", The injured man looked out in the distance seeing Max run toward nothing. "Sophia!", Max called out, seeing a young brunette woman in the distance stumble forward towards the wild-eyed man. "My love! You must come home with us!" He yelled, edging closer by the moment. Tom watched him with caution, *"Something isn't right here, not at all."*, The wind blew harder as he struggled to stand up, trying to view the man in the distance. "Sophia?", Max approached the young brunette woman, her head down and her hair burnt. Clothes torn, soaked and stained with ash. Max reached out for her shoulder, placing his hand on her bony shoulder. The wind blew harder as he watched the woman blow away into dust and dirt. His view blurred as dust flew around, losing his sight of Tom. A figure came out of the whirlwind, a young boy with bloody eyes stood ominously, making Max weep softly. "What do you want from me! I've lost everything, I've done everything I could! What else could you possibly want!", The young boy smiled wide and opened his mouth, his voice raspy and hoarse. "To see the world at its knees, and to see you desperately fail to save it.", Tom covered his face, trying to see through the thick wind, the dust particles burning in his eyes as he stumbled forward. Tom called out, hoping he could find where his partner had disappeared to, but only the wind echoed back. The sounds of screeching erupted to his left causing Tom to turn and look for the source. Yelling was heard in the distance, although he couldn't see anything through the blistering wind. Out of nowhere, Max tore through the cloudy whirlwind, running for his life and waving wildly at Tom. "GO! NOW!", Tom took a moment to comprehend what he had said, as the wind made communication difficult. Then, a massive beast the size of a trailer erupted through the cloud of dirt, darting towards Tom. Its massive claws tore through the wasteland as Tom's feet began to run as fast as he could towards the portal. Max's heart raced wildly, his lungs burning and his legs ached. He glanced back to see the monstrosity edging closer to Tom, swinging wildly in attempts to snatch the man. The portal shone brightly, like the gate to Heaven. Max darted faster as the world shook behind him. "*Almost there, almost there...*", Then the thumping stopped, as a shadow engulfed the two men. Max kept running, hoping to live another day or another minute. Tom stopped and stared up as the beast leaped high in the sky, screeching loudly. It dropped to the ground with ease blocking the portal. Max slowed down, his feet struggling to stop as he now stood a mere few feet from the monstrosity. It swatted at Max knocking him to the dirt, roaring in success. Max groaned quietly, trying to get up as the beast let out a mocking laugh. Raising his head, his eyes full of agony and pure rage. He felt his hands burn as they slowly turned an eerie black. All he could feel was anger and rage, the corruption spreading all over his body. Tom stood back, watching the man slowly rise up off the ground. Truly knowing this might be the end, a tear shed from Tom's left eye, it's once clear color now smeared red. It hit the ground like glass, the water evaporating up into the air.Tom tried to hold back the pain, the anger but it was too much. Falling to his knees, he screamed wildly grasping at his head. Then, the world stopped, Tom stood up with feelings of calm and serenity. Stepping towards the massive creature, his steps were full of certainty. His forehead clear, no beads of sweat poured down his cheek. Only him, only his confidence. Max screamed loudly. "Tom! What are you doing?!", Max tried to move his legs but found himself glued as cold sweat formed across his forehead. The monstrosity laughed horrendously, shaking the ground. Tom only moved closer, face calm and body stiff. The massive beast swung its grotesque claws at Tom, slicing up his body into pieces. No screams, no agony was heard from the man, just the sound of his limbs hitting the ground. Max felt his heart tear into pieces as he fell to the ground in defeat. *"How much more can I lose?"*, Max thought, replaying Tom being shredded to pieces in his mind. The beast roared loudly, its legs vibrated the ground, bringing Max back to reality. He glanced up, it's hideous face dripping a pool of saliva onto the scorched wasteland. Max knew one thing, die here in this desolate world or escape. Rising up to the ground, groaning quietly, he wiped the dust off his kneecaps and stared down the beast. *"Not today, I will not make Tom another worthless sacrifice to this wretched world."* His feet shuffled forward, sweat ran down his face. Max clenched his fists as the beast growled. Picking up his pace, he began to dart towards the portal, the monster racing towards him, thrashing its massive claws at the panicked man. Running faster, his heart raced loudly in his eardrums pushing his body to the limit. Inches from the portal the sound of screeching erupted from above as Max felt tremendous pain in his chest. He looked around only to find himself airborne, flying across the deserted wasteland. With a thud, he fell to the ground. Blood pooled, spilling onto the dirt. Coughing and gasping for air, Max could only see upwards into the orange sky. The sounds of thumps edged closer, the monstrosity ready to finish its prey. A massive pool of saliva slapped down onto the ground next to him as the beast stood over him, tall and menacing. "Get on with it! Kill me!", Max yelled at the beast, wondering why it hesitated. A man slid down the creature's legs, suit and tie with a briefcase in hand. *"Oh, does this guy ever have some day job to do besides ruin mine?"*, Thoughts ran through his head as he immediately recognized the god-like being. "Well, I see you've been enjoying my new *improvements*. You like what I've done with the place? Even got a temple for sacrifices going on now.", Stardust spoke, his tone sarcastic and playful. He paced around, holding on to his fedora as the wind blew harder. Stardust walked over to where Tom laid in pieces, picking up his head and examining it before pitching it aside like garbage. "Such a good friend, too bad he couldn't take it anymore, you know?", Stardust kicked the dust with his polished shoes, his head down. Max laid on the ground, blood still pooling from his chest, coughing and heaving. "I mean, *you* could've saved him, could've *stopped* him, but you just stood there." The man ranted on, taunting Max. "Let me tell you a story, Max.", The bleeding man groaned in pain, trying to get up. "Back before your old man took me to the grave, we used to be good partners, just like you and Tom *were*." Shuffling forward and moaning in pain, Max slowly rose up from the ground, stumbling forward. Blood spilled out of his insides; his vision blurry as he tried to head towards the portal. Stardust continued his story, smiling. "And your mother, man. Your father was a very lucky man.", Max stumbled forward, nearing the portal, his arms reached out, his mind pushing hard to keep moving.", Stardust glanced at the bright star in the sky, unaware of Max's movements. "Too bad she was another pretty whore gone to *waste*.", The dying man stopped in his tracks, and turned. "What did you just call my mother?", Max quietly spoke, his tone hushed underlying massive amounts of rage. "I mean, why else do you think he 'accidentally' pushed me into a portal and trapped me for decades? The Burrows Family has always had some *temper issues*." Max stepped forward ignoring the pain of his deadly wounds, only focused on Stardust. "Don't call my mother that.", Max clenched his fists, feeling the rage rise up through his throat. "Don't call my mother that!", Stardust mocked him, laughing as he settled the briefcase lightly on the dirt. The godly being crackles his knuckles and murmured, "This should be easy." Max ran towards the man wildly, focusing his anger towards inflicting any possible harm onto his tormentor. Stardust turned his back and snapped his fingers, chuckling to himself. The god then felt the weight of a train hit me, throwing him off the ground. Hitting the ground hard, he tumbled into the dry dirt. "Man, this is my nice suit. You got a tear in it!", Max continued walking forward, the corruption spreading onto his arms. His vision blurred as his arms turned a deep black, his mind only hearing one thing. Rage. Heat seared his body, feeling like flames from hell itself. "Look at you, all grown up! My beautiful creation. I had my doubts but you came out just great, just look at yourself!", the god laughed, maintaining his sarcastic tone. "Just like your *father*.", Stardust taunted the man once again. Max glanced down at his hands and arms, once a tan now was an unnatural black.

"I-I, I gave in. I let this power control me.", Max stuttered, realizing what he had done. "No, I can't let you have control again, I. Don't want this power.", the man continued, trying to understand what he had done. His hands slowly faded into its original tan color as his vision lightened and his head cleared. "No!", Stardust screamed loudly, shaking his head. "You have no control over me.", Max stated, making his stance firm on the ground. "So be it.", The god-being raised his hand, levitating Max off the ground and swung his hand, flinging Max through the portal. "I'll see you soon, *friend.*", Max slid across the dirt, head dragging into the cold soil. Vision blurred, he rose his head off the cold dirt and saw someone approach him. Max quickly shuffled backwards in panic, grabbing the bark on the side of the tree behind me. "Get away!" The poor man screamed, as the figure edged closer. The figure came into the light, revealing himself to Max. "H-how, you died! I watched you get torn to pieces!", Tom smiled, reaching a hand to the man. "He told me to tell you it's a homecoming gift, whatever that means.", The two men turned back to the machine which had been heavily damaged due to the activation, wondering what to do now. "If there was some way, we could open the portal up at a different time point in our dimension, we could save the city before the events we witnessed take place.", Max explained. Tom glanced down at the machine before glancing up at the starless sky. "We'll need time, and we don't have much. Silent Falls needs us Max. If we don't get out of here, then the whole world is gone. There is no failure as an option, only success.", Max sighed quietly and held his stomach where wounds used to be. "Then let's get to work."

Sophia walked hand in hand with Max, entering the hallway quietly. Her elegant red dress sparkled as she neared the entrance to the party. Max walked beside her, his grey suit and tie without wrinkle or blemish. Sophia reached for the doorknob and let out a quiet sigh. In her mind, she knew what lay behind the door. Hundreds of careless, oblivious people. They didn't know the secrets she kept. They wouldn't believe her. They wouldn't dare accuse let alone even think that her husband was a dark cosmic entity controlling them all, manipulating them, their emotions, their will. All they knew was the man, the hero of the day, their glorious leader. A man without blemish, wrinkle. Their savior. The door opened as hundreds of people stood around the massive ballroom in expensive suits and fabulous dresses. The entire city was invited here, all their eyes watching the couple entering the room as the chatter died down focusing their attention on them. Gasps from the crowd and whistles erupted through the crowd as she walked through the parted crowd in the revealing dress, her eyes sparkled like an angel. As they ascended the stairs to the podium, Sophia wanted to reach for the knife hidden under heel and slash right at the man's back. She could only imagine the blood spurting out of the back of his neck, falling to the floor in pain. She could see her face smeared with blood, the knife in her hand trembling violently. And then, she would turn to the crowd and announce the testimony she'd been hiding for months. The crowd would cheer her name as a hero and she could be free from her burden, her fear of being one of his next victims. Snapping out of her fantasy, she quickly stepped up behind Max smiling as nothing had happened, her fist clenched and her smile trembling. Max began to speak elegantly, his voice smooth and professional. *"No wonder everyone is so drawn to his lies."*, Sophia thought, her eyes focused on the crowd below them. Max continued speaking, knowing his words were having his desired effect on the crowd. "Today, we celebrate 5 years of peace! This day makes us proud, why?", Max hesitated, knowing he was lying to the public, but he smiled anyway. Besides, deception was his favorite weapon. "Because five years ago, on this very day. We defeated God himself. He came down from the heavens, promising peace if we only bowed down on our knees!", The crowd booed loudly, Max chuckled at the crowd, knowing they could never defeat a god, let alone him. "But not just I, but all of us stood up united against his false promises! And we defeated the god!", the crowd roared in applause and cheering, Sophia only rolled her eyes in disbelief, she knew the truth. She glanced down at her hands which were covered in blood, the knife in her hand. The back of Max's neck spurting out blood. Then she rubbed her eyes wiping the eyeshadow partially off her eye and looked back at her hands, polished and clean. The speech ended as Max stepped away from the podium, bringing his hand onto her shoulder. "Sophia, are you feeling alright? You've been acting strange since we got here.", Max asked, the sound of worry in his voice. She knew he didn't care for her; all this was an act. She felt the rage boil up in her throat, ready to end it all. To end the madness, his reign of terror. But she knew she couldn't. She quietly breathed out, calming down and smiled into his brightly colored green eyes. "Yes, I'm alright my honey boo.", She placed her hand on his arm lightly touching it. "And if you don't mind my dear, I'll be getting a drink.", Max smiled at her, his 'worry' disappearing in a flash. Glad she wasn't suspecting anything, he knew she had to be rid of somehow but not now, he had plans for her. Sophia quickly hurried through the crowd, feeling the vomit rise like a volcano inside her throat. Several people called her name out, wanting to speak to the lady of the night. She quickly pushed the door into the hallway, running in her flats to the bathroom. Sophia pushed open the door, rushing to the sink, her throat full of bile. She immediately vomited in the marble sink, staining it with a tan mixture. She rose her head out of the sink staring at the reflection in the mirror with disgust. Slowly reaching for the small dagger under her foot, her eyes focused on her reflection. Sophia felt the dagger in her hand slowly inch closer to her neck, slowly cutting deeper and deeper into it. *"I can't let him get away with this again."*, The door swung open and a young woman entered, her dress a bright blue and sparkly. "Oh hey Mrs. Burrow-, Oh my! What are you doing to yourself?", The woman asked, in shock at the blood that spilled on the floor. Sophia turned to her, stunned. "You don't understand...I can't live with him anymore! I can't escape that evil being!", Sophia screamed, tears rolling down her eyes, staining her makeup. "Darling, what are you talking about, let me go get some bandages and we can talk ab- ",the woman was cut off as Sophia's face turned a bright red, her anger and frustration spilling out. "You don't understand. If He finds out, he'll kill me!", her eyes watered up again ready to burst like a waterfall. "Now you're just making no sense, Mr. Burrows would never hurt a fly. Come on, let's go get you cleaned up and relax.", the woman said, her voice calm and soothing. Turning away with intentions of exiting the bathroom, Sophia felt the rage boil up inside, that anger roaring loudly inside her head. Screeching loudly with rage, darting towards the woman, dagger in hand. She slammed the dagger into the back of the woman's neck, blood spurting into Sophia's face. The woman screamed in terror collapsing to the ground. Standing over the limp body, the dagger dripped wildly with blood. "No one can know. No one.", Looking into the mirror, she saw Max staring back at her smiling. Sophia laughed, blood-stained tears rolling down her pale face. It was only a matter of time before she would lose herself to the madness and corruption.

Marcus gazed up at the massive rocket in awe. Sparks flew off, grinding at the metal. "How long til it's ready for evacuation?", Marcus asked, his eyes locked on the rocket. "My lord, the rocket is nearly operational but I'm afraid the lunar base will not be fully restored until at least a month from now.", The engineer spoke, his body shivered in fear. Marcus shook his head, breaking his long gaze at the rocket. His eyes settled on the small man, glaring at him with hatred. "You have three weeks. We cannot afford any longer.", Marcus demanded, his hands waved to express his anger. "If you don't mind me asking, what is this all for, my lord?", The engineer's voice was frail, his eyes struggling to meet Marcus. "Are you questioning me? I built this empire and you question my actions?", He roared, his eyes were blazed with rage. "No, sir. I-I, I was just curious on why you were so urg-.", The engineer tried to explain, his eyes were wide with fear.

Marcus turned, looking back up at the rocket. "All you need to know is to trust me.", His voice lowered. The engineer saluted frantically before scurrying off to a workstation. Sighing, his hands reached out, touching the metal fin. It's cold touch was a reminder of his past. Marcus walked towards the rusted elevator. It lowered, letting out a ring, signaling the opening of the doors. He stepped inside the elevator alone. It quickly let out a creak, shutting the doors. "Leaving so soon, Marcus?", the man appeared in the other corner of the elevator. His familiar voice caused Marcus to grab his dagger, backing against the metal cage. "Such a welcoming greeting. Primitive tools must be your expertise?", The man let out a chuckle, his emerald eyes gazing at Marcus. "Demon! We drove you back into the portal. How did you escape?", Marcus held the knife close to his chest, prepared to defend. "Centuries locked in a cage. I found the truth; I exploited its power.

I waited for the foolish souls to open the Gateway. Mr. Burrows didn't suffer too long, I suppose.", Stardust explained. Marcus glared at the being with hatred, "You shall leave my city alone, you demon.", He watched Stardust laugh for a moment before returning to his blank look. "This time. There won't be any cities left.", Stardust laughed maniacally, his laughter taunting Marcus. Sunlight peered in from the metal openings, the doors of the elevator swung open. In a blink of an eye, Stardust was gone. Marcus stepped outside; the bright evening sun shone on his pale skin. "Three weeks.",

Sophia sat at the desk, anxious and sweating nervously as the front door closed downstairs. **Tick tock.** "Honey, I'm home!". Max yelled from the living room downstairs. "I'm up here love, in the office!", / "How was work?", Sophia asked, trying to maintain her fake smile, as she shifted nervously in the chair. The tension in her voice strained further. "It was good, but are you alright? You seem tense.", Max frowned and looked at her with worry in his eyes. "It's just..I haven't felt too good for a few days.", Sophia lied and smiled nervously at him, she tapped her foot anxiously. He was on to her, he had to know. "Honey, go to bed dear, you look like you're about to have a heart attack.", Max said with a saddened tone. Sophia got up and reached in for a hug, *It almost felt real, it almost felt like him.* She smiled at Max and headed towards the bedroom. Shuffling around the bed, she settled in and held on the sheets tight. An hour passed before Max settled into bed beside her and quickly slipped into deep sleep. Another hour passed as sweat poured down her forehead. Tick, tock the clock chimed the midnight hour. Sophia shifted in the bed and slowly creeped out of the bed and out of the bedroom. Drops of sweat poured off her forehead and hit the floor, like bullets bouncing off a shield. Sophia opened the door and slipped through. She quietly tiptoed down the stairs as the anxiety rose within her. *What if she got caught? What am I going to say? No, I gotta think positive, stay positive.* She stepped down into the dark basement and turned the light on. *Tick, tock.* The clock clicked back and forth like a bomb about to detonate. She reached under the sink and pressed the hidden button, the wall shifted and a chest appeared. Sophia quickly opened the chest and grabbed the book, opening it to examine the details. She quickly closed the book and turned around only to find Max standing there. "What are you doing? You're not going anywhere with that, are you?", Max asked, his eyes stone cold on her. "I.. -I-I", Sophia tried to speak but no words could come out, her heart froze and she couldn't move. "Oh sweetheart, you really think I didn't know?", Max smiled. "Well, I-I, I didn't know th-ht.", Sophia continued to stutter. "You really think I let you plan our anniversary without me?", Max laughed and smiled at her. *No, no I was right! He didn't expect anything.* Sophia relaxed and smiled back at him, everything seemed okay. "Come on, let's get some sleep.", Max said and the two ascended the stairs. She began walking up the stairs and started to feel dizzy, her heart pounded like it was going to explode, something felt like it was constricting her throat. Max smiled at her and said, "You really think I didn't know? You were such a pretty woman, so sad Max never got to enjoy it.", Sophia struggled to breathe and tried to speak, "Y-you'll never get away with t-this.", Stardust laughed at her comment and replied, "I'm sure all it will be is just a *heart attack.*", The world spun around and her heart exploded as she fell to the floor. Then the world went black. The last thing she heard was, "See you soon."

The young reporter looked at the article and frowned, the contents laid out before her.

"Sophia Burrows was found dead in the Burrows' Estate around December 30th, 2024. Reports say Mr. Burrows called around Eleven PM at night saying she couldn't breathe, and woke up abruptly mid-sleep. Mr. Burrows said she was acting weird and seemed on edge throughout the day before going to bed. "I just wish I knew; I wish I could've said goodbye.", A quote provided by Mr. Burrows. A funeral will be planned around January 3rd, all who can attend please do, this was such a tragic death. All our prayers go to Mr. Burrows in this tragic situation. Stay strong, Silent Falls."

She slammed her fist down hard on the desk in frustration. Sophia was her only informant she had in this case. *"Did I get her killed?"*, Alexis thought to herself, her anxiety raising higher and higher by each moment. Alexis had been investigating this case for a year now, hoping to uncover what really happened in the 'Battle of the Stars' as they nicknamed it. Sophia had come to her with enticing evidence to prove her claim, but was hesitant to give it to her. Everyone seemed so much happier than before, like they wanted her dead. Like *He* wanted her dead. Alexis reached over and turned on the computer, the Stardust Inc. logo appearing on the monitor. The computer hummed quietly as she tapped her foot anxiously under the desk. "Pretty tragic, isn't it.", one of her coworkers walked up behind her, staring at the news story of Sophia's death. "Yeah…she was a good friend to me, the sweetest person alive.",

Alexis replied, slowly sliding the folder full of evidence under the article to hide it from her coworkers. "Well, the whole news team is planning on going to the funeral, it's Thursday at Five PM." Her co-worker said, her voice with sorrow. "I'll...try to be there." Alexis sighed, hoping her co-worker would leave. With a pat on the shoulder and the sound of retreating footsteps she was left alone at her desk once again. Alexis began to type her new article called, "Mayor or Liar?", she reached down and opened up the folder of evidence and began to type once more. *"I'm going to expose this man once for all."*, Alexis thought to herself, she cracked her knuckles and smiled. Furious typing continued for an hour and she finally sat back in her chair smiling at the masterpiece. *"Friday, I'll make sure Silent Falls knows who they really look up to, an evil being."* The sounds of her editor's voice followed by a very familiar voice entered the large office room. She quickly closed the document and sat upright as the Editor and the man came closer, speaking indistinctly. Alexis turned to see her Editor and the man she had just been writing about, the mayor himself. Her face turned a deep red and she put on her fake smile. "Mr. Burrows, I'd like you to meet one of our finest writers on the news team. Alexis Brighton.", Max smiled at her and reached out for a handshake. Alexis hesitated; her heart raced. Alexis snapped back to reality, and rapidly reached to handshake the man. "I'm so sorry, I-I... I-I mean, it's an honor to meet you, Mayor Burrows.", She stammered, her face hot and red. "It's fine, I get the same look all the time.", Max said, his smile beaming a sense of calmness and unreal serenity. "I-I'm so sorry about your loss, your wife was an amazing person. I worked with her quite a lot in getting that museum restored.", Alexis stuttered more, still blushing a deep red tone. The man was remarkably handsome and she almost felt herself lost in his evergreen eyes. "Yeah. I remember Sophia speaking about you once or twice."

Alexis blushed; her heart raced faster. "Well, it's an honor to meet *you, Ms. Brighton*. I hope to see you at the funeral.", Max's charm radiated off, making her feel so at ease. Alexis giggled and waved slowly as Max and the Editor turned to walk away. Still in a daze, smiling ear to ear, all she could think of was his beautiful evergreen eyes. She snapped out of her daze standing up from the chair, grabbing the folder and quickly exiting the building. If she knew anything, she would end that monster as soon as possible.

James stood at the door, smiling and greeting people as they walked into the church. The solemn faces and some, crying faces were seen as most of the townspeople entered. The funeral was today and James had really seen no real reason to be there besides publicity and his reputation. *"After all, Max is the one that killed her anyway."*, James thought, having planned this out with Max. He began to close the door when a young woman rushed in, notebook in hand. She smiled at him briefly and quickly took a seat. James closed the door to the church and stood, towering over the crowd. The man himself stood at the podium, solemn and neutral. Max looked around at the crowd, eager to get started. "Ahem, it's a sad day in Silent Falls.", Max started, putting on his best act. "We lost someone valuable to u-us all. She was a star to me, a beacon of hope.", Max stuttered, trying to fool the crowd with his soap opera. "We all miss her, I miss her hugs, I miss how she m-made me smi-.", Max stuttered once more, then stopped abruptly. "J-just. I need a m-moment.", He began to weep, hot tears slowly dripping down his cheek. One woman in the crowd began to sob loudly, causing the crowd to turn somber. Josh sat in the crowd, rolling his eyes at the woman's response. "Ladies and gentlemen, I'd like Mr. Salem to speak a few words.", Max spoke, as James signaled a thumbs down and possessed a confused look on his face. Max's face beaming, trying to put on a good show. James sighed deeply trying to express his annoyance by this. He stepped forward through the pews, putting on his fake smile. The crowd shifted, turning to look up at the towering man as he headed towards the front. Faces full of sadness and a grim reality. James stepped up on the podium, the old wooden stairs creaking. He glanced around, scanning the crowd and saw Sophia sitting in the back pew, smiling as blood dripped down cheek. James shivered and looked down to try to find the right words to say. "I didn't know Sophia very well but from what Sta-, ahem Max told me, she was the most wonderful person you could meet. Her crimson- her ocean blue eyes, reminded me of my sister, if only we could cherish the dead longer, thank you.", James quickly left the podium, rushing down the stairs. Max stepped up and smiled at the crowd, "Thank you all for coming. Have a wonderful weekend. Thank you again.", Max spoke softly, dismissing the crowd as James slowly exited the building with them. The road was quiet and eerie, the sun setting. A crunch of a branch echoed through the woods, causing James to turn around and look for the culprit, and stood defensively. He turned back only to jump back in shock. "Will you be there tonight?", Stardust questioned him, leaning against the tree. "Yes, I wouldn't miss it for nothing. Our work is almost finished.", James replied, his eyes struggling to meet the man's face. "Seven. It's essential that you be there.", Stardust spoke, his tone concerning. With a quick flash, the man disappeared in a cloud of black smoke. His legs picked up speed, sprinting towards his house. Minutes later, he arrived at the massive mansion. He opened the tall, spruce doors. Rushing into the kitchen, he swung open the refrigerator door. Grabbing the bottle of champagne, he rushed out the door towards the laboratory. His eyes glistened with celebration.

Alexis sat in her editor's office quietly waiting for him to get back with the coffee. She tapped her foot anxiously, knowing she awaited her demise. Her face bloodshot red with embarrassment and shame. Alexis knew she had messed up majorly. But she also knew that she released the truth. She had seen the reviews and complaints and wasn't surprised. Denial is one of the first steps in the process of accepting such a culture shock. *"I'm getting fired for revealing the truth? Why am I embarrassed with my decisions? Shouldn't I feel proud of what I've done? Exposed an entire empire of lies and corruption?"*, Alexis thought deeply. The door swung open behind her and the sound of shades being closed was heard. Her boss Tim, walked around the desk and sat down in the chair, his eyes full of fury and rage. His hand shook with anger as the coffee sloshed in the cup. Tim sat the cup down and put his hands together, putting on the fakest smile she had ever seen. In the calmest voice she had heard, he began to speak. "Ms. Brighton, your actions recently, especially with your latest *project* have been reckless and extremely unprofessional.", His voice tightening, trying to remain professional. His face was red with anger, and she knew what she had done. "Do you have any idea what you've done? The damage you've done to our reputation?", Tim asked, his voice full of anger. She tapped her fingers on the desk, her anxiety rising. She only nodded her head in response to his questions. "Do you have any *comments* on your recent actions?", The man's face got redder by the moment. She could see the veins popping out of his forehead. His hand still trembled and slowly formed to a fist. She slowly scooted back and sat upright in her chair. Smiling at the man, she prepared her response. "Sir, I know my actions have been quite unprofessional but as my duty as a reporter, I'm morally obligated to speak the truth, even the most shocking things should be presented to the public and not hidden in lies." She smiled even more watching the man foam at the mouth in anger. His hand slammed on the desk causing the coffee to splash onto the desk. "YOU ACTUALLY BELIEVE THIS GARBAGE?", Tim screamed, losing all form of professionalism. He foamed at the mouth, spurting out anything and trying to find words to describe his rage. Alexis only sat there and smiled at the man, "I do, my job is to uncover the tru-,", Alexis was quickly cut off as Tim screamed once more, "YOU RUINED THIS COMPANY, YOU RUINED MY DREAM.", He screamed louder and louder, swinging his hands in the air to demonstrate his fury. The coffee was dumped over in the process, staining the paperwork on the desk, steaming like Tim. "I CAN'T BELIEVE THIS, LORD STARDUST WON'T BE HAPPY WITH THIS.", Tim screamed even louder, the room full of employees were still, listening to the man screaming. "What did you say?", Alexis asked, hearing the name of a familiar individual. Tim growled, "THE

MAYOR ISN'T GOING TO BE HAPPY. NOW GET OUT!", Alexis quickly wrote the name down and hurried out of the office. Her head down as her former co-workers stared at her in shock. She quickly exited the room and headed out the building. The sky was eerie gray, people seemed to notice her and point, calling her a "fraud" and more derogatory names. She quickly hurried down the street, heading home. The wind blew hard and a heat like a fire burning was felt as she neared her home. She lifted her head and saw the burning smoke in the distance. She began to run quickly towards her house. The smoke only got thicker as she coughed more. Then it cleared and she finally saw where the fire originated. The fire came from her house, which was intentionally set on fire. Alexis felt her knees go weak; the cold tears burst from her eyes. She fell to her knees, dropping her things. "Everything, I-I worked for, I did is…. GONE." Alexis stuttered; her face covered with tears of sorrow. "It was all because of that stupid ARTICLE!", Alexis screamed, her sorrow and pain slowly turning into hatred and fury. She slammed her head into the concrete sidewalk feeling the pain rush to her head and the dizziness began its onslaught. Blood dripped from her forehead as she laid her head on the concrete sidewalk crying his eyes out. She reached up and felt the wound bleeding Wiley, her hands now coated in blood. "It's all over for me, I ruined everything…", She cried, smearing the blood into her rosy tear-stained cheeks. Alexis had lost everything, her career, her dreams and her sanity. What felt like hours, she finally rose from the concrete sidewalk and stumbled forward, her hands and face stained from the blood. The wound on her forehead dried up, slowly stopping the stream of blood running into her eyes. All she knew at that point was that she had to fix things and make everything okay. She stumbled and walked, vision blurry and mind hazy to The Burrows Estate. People stared at her as she walked, her face stained with blood. They stared at her with horror, looking at the person she had turned herself into. All she knew was to keep walking, to fix everything. The bright lights of the mansion shone elegantly in the evening sky emitting an aura around the home. She stepped closer to the small porch, stumbling and tripping.

Reaching the door, it's grand entrance to the mansion seemed luxurious to her. She pressed the doorbell button ringing throughout the house. The sound of movement from the kitchen and the clash of dishes was heard as footsteps neared closer to the door. She stood up straight and wiped the tears off her face. The door swung open as she looked up at the man himself, wearing a suit and tie. He glanced at her in confusion for a moment and then smiled, "I-I ca-,", before she could speak, he motioned her in with a smile. "I knew you would come to apologize.", Max said, his smile emitting a sense of kindness that warmed her heart. "Please, I prepared for your arrival.", Max motioned for her to sit at the elegant table, it's finest wood shining against the golden chandelier above. The golden silverware sat next to the silver plate, reflecting off the plate. Max left the room and entered the kitchen, leaving her alone in the dining room. She glanced around, quite confused by his welcoming approach. Max entered with a plate of the juiciest meat she had ever seen. He sat the plate on the table and only kept his smile. Max pulled the chair back and sat down. She knew something was off, no one would just invite her into their home especially looking like that. "Why are you doing this?", She blurted out, then sunk back in her chair realizing how rude it sounded. "Because, forgiveness of your greatest fans is the key to salvation, and you, my poor citizen, are in need of some salvation.", Max replied, his tone soft and humble. She stared at the man as he began to eat, looking at his emerald eyes. Then snapped out of her gaze and looked down at the plate. Her bloody hands grabbed the silver and she slowly began to eat. Enjoying the food, she was overwhelmed with a sense of euphoria. She eagerly grabbed more of the food and began to eat faster. "This is really good, where di-," Alexis began to raise her head to speak to Max but he was nowhere to be found. She glanced around the room searching for the man. The flame of a cigarette flashed in the corner of the room and the sound of footsteps nearing closer was heard. A tall man wearing a fedora and a grey suit and tie stepped out of the shadows ominously. She stared at the man's emerald eyes and scooted back in her chair, confused and felt the anxiety in her body rise. He stepped forward and sat down in the chair where Max once sat. The man stared at the young woman and smiled for a moment, lasting a minute of silence. "Ahem, I suppose you have many questions about my presence here." The man spoke, his voice rough and he sat the cigarette on the table, the ashes still burning. Alexis stared at the man with a startled look, afraid of what he might do to her. "Where is…Max?", Alexis asked, fork in hand where she was once eating. The man smiled wider and tapped his foot quietly. "You know who I am, Alexis.", The man said, prompting her to think. "How do you know my n-name..?"Alexis stammered, obviously frightened by the man's knowledge of her. He laughed loudly. "It isn't hard to figure names, especially when you wrote everything about me in the newspaper.", The man smiled, "I'm everywhere.", the man disappeared from the chair as she looked around to see where he went. "I'm right here,", he whispered in her ear, causing her to jump back violently. "Y-you, h-h did y-yo,", She was at a loss of words, then the man appeared back in the chair, his hands clasped together. "I've come to make a deal, Alexis. I particularly don't like things getting in my way, but today, I'm feeling generous.", Stardust explained, his tone deepening. "What do you desire the most?", He asked Alexis, smiling, knowing how this was going to end. She felt her rage and anger from today's events bottle up. She hated her boss; she hated this town. The way he treated her. "I desire…", Alexis paused, thinking about the rage, the anger she felt. "I desire to see my boss to feel the pain I endured…", Stardust laughed at her request, *"Such a small goal,"*, he thought. He reached out his hand to signal the end of the deal, and she gladly shook his hand. The darkness pulsed violently through her veins as she shook his hand. She let go and felt herself feel dizzy. "As you wish,", Stardust pointed his finger towards the door as the man she wished revenge for appeared. Mr. Eddleton appeared, covered in blood. He screamed out in pain, blood poured across his forehead, making a pool of blood pour onto the floor. He screamed for help as Stardust laughed, the man felt his skin burn. His pores began to ooze blood. "Help…", he whimpered, staring at Alexis. His eyes full of fear as he cried for help. Alexis only stared back at the man smiling. She felt the heat of darkness increase and she embraced it. Stardust looked at Alexis and smiled, clearly enjoying seeing her smile at the withering man. The man's eyes bulged out of its sockets and he fell limp on the floor as his skin withered away. Stardust looked at Alexis once again, "Shall we begin the transformation, my darling?", He asked softly, Alexis felt her body burning in pain and only smiled, "I believe I'm ready.", the darkness brewed faster and faster, spreading through her mind. "The portal is almost complete; I think it's time I did some *redecorating*."

James arrived at the laboratory, champagne in hand. He smiled; the bottle was half empty. "I brought some celebratory drinks to enjoy.", James laughed, drunk. Stardust frowned; his annoyance clearly stated in his looks. "Mr. Salem, I wish you took this matter more seriously.", James stumbled across the room, taking another swig of the bottle. "More for me then!", He shouted, leaning against the concrete walls of the laboratory. He glanced over at the young woman, squinting his eyes. "Why is she here?", His words were slurred, but still understandable. "She's our test subject.", Stardust guided the woman inside the containment chamber, closing it shut behind her. James watched curiously as the woman smiled, her eyes were glazed over. The alarms rang out, initiating the activation. The spark ignited. His hands trembled with a sense of fear as the portal activated. It shone its eerie glow onto the girl. Her laughter was hysterical. James watched in horror as the laughter turned into screaming. Her skin ripped, the oozing black substance erupted from the open wounds, rising like tentacles. His stomach moaned in disgust, the bile rising like a fire in his throat. "It's wonderful, isn't it.", The voice rang through his ears, the tone was joyful, not urgent and disgusted. "I need to go to the restroom.", James began to walk towards the exit, his heart sinking. Stardust's hand gripped his shoulder firmly. He felt the heat burning at his skin. "You weren't going to skip out on the show, were you?", James shuffled his feet around, smiling. "Of course not, I can surely wait another five minutes.", His voice tightened, trying to smile genuinely. His feet shifted back towards the containment window. Alexis stood inside, the tendrils ripping through her skin rapidly. Her screams mixed in with laughter. *"Is she enjoying this?"*, His expression was full of fear. Stardust laughed, giving him chills. The containment door shifted and creaked. Alexis was out of his view. He stepped closer to the glass, his eyes darting across the containment room. The door began to let out a loud creak. His heart sank. His body turned to back up, but his legs were frozen. Stardust only smiled wider, tears running down his face. The door bent off the brackets, flying across the room. James ducked instinctively. The door phased through Stardust who didn't move an inch. James peeked at the doorway, trying to find Alexis. The black tendrils poked out of her body; her eyes were stained with blood. He let it all go, the bile spilled out of his mouth. He coughed, spitting on the ground. "My creation...", Stardust wept, his voice full of joy. James slowly stepped back, edging closer to the elevator. "Mr. Salem. I believe it is our time. Now my powers are fully restored, I will finish our deal.", James tried to move. His feet shifted back and forth trying to run. But all he could do is watch in fear. The familiar burning pain spiked in his chest. His hands trembled immensely. James tried to scream, but his lungs burned harder with every breath. His shoulder twitched rapidly flinging his arms everywhere. His skin peeled, the corruption spreading across his body. Groaning in pain, the tendrils reached out of his mouth. They wrapped around his body like cable, covering James completely. James tried to breathe; his heart raced faster. Stardust laughed maniacally watching the man silently scream in pain. "This is what you wanted right? To be a god?", Stardust taunted. The tendrils enveloped his body, Like the wind, everything settled. He felt calm. He felt *powerful*. His new form was heinous, an unbearable sight but powerful. He could feel the power course through his veins. James began to levitate. He busted out of the laboratory, his laughter echoing across the park.

Marcus scanned the room. His eyes gazed at the crowd; their faces full of confusion. The soldiers ushered the crowd into the rocket. Their bags were filled with clothes, food and accessories. He yelled, urging them to move faster. "How long do we have before the event occurs?", He asked, his voice was quiet. His eyebrows were furrowed. "Mr. Time should be here any minute with the signal.", Dwaine explained. Marcus paced. He could feel the dread rising in his heart. The yelling erupted from the middle of the crowd. The man beat at the soldier pinning down to the floor. Marcus quickly ran over investigating the scene. He yelled menacingly. Both of them looked up, backing away. Sighing, he raised his pistol. He fired two shots, ringing into his ears. The man and the guard fell to the floor, their corpses were still. "Anyone else want to start issues?", He called out, raising his weapon in the air. The crowd quickly shuffled towards the entrance of the rocket. "Have we got the signal yet?", Marcus swiftly pivoted to face Dwaine. "Nothing yet. I expected him to be here by now.", Marcus groaned. He lowered his head, thinking. "Marcus, we must leave now. The seismograph is picking up massive spikes. It's not long before he gains full control.", Dwaine explained, the urgency of his voice was clear. "Make the right choice, brother.",

Max watched the dark star-less sky brighten as flashes of blue light streaked across the sky. Tom rushed out of the small shelter in curiosity, eager to see what could possibly happen in this desolate place. The sky flashed brightly a final time and the sounds of screams echoed across the land. Then, like nothing had ever occurred, the sky went back to its eerie bleak mood. Max glanced up again, then shrugged his shoulders, confused by the bright lights. "What was that? Some kind of light show to taunt us?", Tom stepped forward, still glancing at the bleak, eerie sky, hoping that it meant something, a small glimmer of hope in an empty world. Max shook his head in frustration, slamming his fists into the nearby tree, punching hard as he could. His knuckles bleed a dark bubbling substance in response, oozing down his hand and dripping rapidly onto the ground. Max's hand trembled violently, wondering how far he'd gone. He'd been here for months, maybe even years and had been taunted by the world around him. Clenching his fists, Max began to punch himself in the face as hard as he could. The first punch was brutal, the dark blood smeared across his pale cheeks. The second hit harder, his vision blurry and his head hazy. The sound of Stardust's voice in his head rang out, taunting and sneering at him. "You were destined to fail.", the phrase echoed loudly, the tone full of envy. "Get out of my head!", Max screamed loudly, scratching and clawing at his head to stop the voices. Falling down to his knees, he begged and pleaded for them to stop but the voices only intensified. Mocking him as he screamed in pain and agony. "So much pain, please, just please make it stop.", Max pleaded, trying to find some sort of relief. A soft voice interrupted his pleading as he looked up to see Sophia standing over him, smiling. "My poor dear. Max, you have suffered so much. How about we go home and have a nice dinner tonight?", Max's whimpering stopped as he looked at her in disbelief. His face turned to pure rage, the figure that stood before him was just a taunt. Another way to torment him here in this hellish nightmare. Max swung his fists at the mocking figure, it's body shattering like glass. The shards of its mirror-like reflection were splattered across the ground, reflecting a version of himself that he would never see. A happy man, with kids. A perfect life. "It's quite intriguing to see the effects of this place manifest on humans.", a man's voice rang out, echoing off the trees. "Oh, the corruption of one's mind. How the corrupted bring power to those who have been casted out, trapped in this powerhouse.", the man continued as Stardust appeared out of thin air, slowly drifting to the ground. His dark grey suit shimmered dimly creating an eerie aura around himself. "I was once casted out to this place, trapped for decades. My village sought to banish me because I exploited the power of darkness. But they couldn't control me. They brought in the best of armies the world could see, they all failed. My destiny to rule and eradicate the weak only grew stronger.", Max shifted, his eyes full of rage as Stardust stepped closer. "However, there was one man. A man in particular, who dabbled in these dark arts. He sought to trap me in this solace. And as you know, he did. Who thought by doing that, he'd only create a being of immense power.", Stardust put his finger up to his chin, thinking, a smile on his face? "Who knew his son would be the one to let me out?", Stardust laughed, shaking his head. Max slowly put his head down in shame, knowing he was the one who caused this madness and chaos. "Ah good times, good times we had." Tom creeped out behind the tree, glancing at the two. "Ah yes, the partner.", Tom glared at the god-like being, feelings full of fear and anger. He screamed wildly, rushing towards Stardust, his body full of adrenaline and rage. Stardust laughed and snapped his fingers in amusement, watching Tom turn into ash. Tom's screams for help faded slowly as he tumbled into the ground, the wind blowing the remnants of his body away. Max stood there frozen, his mouth agape and his body in shock. Stardust glanced down at his watch, carelessly wasting time watching Max breakdown in a frenzy of madness. "Ooh, sorry about your friend there.", The being's watch beeped loudly, bringing his attention back to the golden watch. "Well, I suppose I should get going. I got a firework show to see.", He walked away, portal opening as Max took a run for it towards him. He dove through the portal landing behind God's feet. Stardust glanced down at the man who laid bruised on the dirt, "I suppose you could stay for the show, just to prove how worthless and powerless you are to stop any of this.", He raised his hands in the air, ground shaking as the sound of engines firing up. "Welcome to Silent Falls, Max."

Josh ran, his face was a cherry red. His body ached with pain. His legs begged him to stop running. But he couldn't. The ground shook hard, rumbling. He collapsed to the ground, crawling towards the massive field. He could hear the engines fire up. The roar of the rocket preparing to launch. His fingers dug into the dirt. Pulling himself, his body pleaded for him to stop. The launching bay doors rose, exposing the rocket to the open sky. Josh continued to crawl; his hands were stained with mud. The dust cloud exploded out of the bay. He shielded his eyes to the annihilating wind. It rose, the heat blasting at his skin. The hot tears evaporated off his cheek. Josh slammed his head into the ground in distraught, the sobbing muted by the rocket engines above. His head lifted; his hands were frozen. The engines had stopped. Looking up, his eyes saw the rocket split in half. At first glance, he thought the first stage boosters were separating. His legs lifted from the ground in unison, running towards the nearest form of shelter. Up above him, the pieces of the rocket rained down in the distance. The explosion slowly fading. His hands shook, trembling with confusion and fear. He looked back up to the sky; searching for the source. The figure descended towards the ground causing Josh to hide behind the small tree. Peering closer, the man was grotesque. Tendrils poked out of his skin. His hands were rotten, the flesh flaking off. "No more time for hide and seek, Mr. Time." The tree was sliced in half, its branches snapped instantly. Leaving Josh without cover, he began to cower down. "I suppose you're out of time.", James laughed at his pun, his demonic voice phasing in and out. "James. Surely, we can talk about this...", Josh pleaded with the man, his hands held up in defense. "I don't think I'd really want to.", James shrugged his shoulders, his smile was grotesque. Josh shifted back; his body trembled in fear. "You could've been a god! You could've been like me. No more limitations. Nothing could stop you. But now here you are, cowering down to your new god. So pathetic...", James ranted on. The blast knocked James down to the ground, disoriented. Josh frantically looked around, clearly confused. Marcus stepped over James, holding a small rail gun. "It's time to go.", Marcus called out, motioning him. The bright sun seemed to dim with every minute that passed. Josh ran along the road; the trees were stripped bare. Ashes rained down like snowflakes. Smoke pillars rose high in the sky in the distance. In the distance, the walls of the city were in ruins, ripped apart. His legs were burning, trying to keep up with the older man. Marcus slowed down, examining the carnage. "My god! It's worse than I expected.", Marcus exclaimed. Josh gazed at the blood splattered across the brick building. The corpses laid strewn across the road, their mouths agape. "Why would someone want so much death, so...much chaos, His question emerged from his mouth abruptly. Marcus stopped dead still. He turned to face Josh, who's eyes struggled to meet him. "Corruption is a powerful tool. What was once pure and holy.", Marcus paused, turning to look at the lifeless bodies on the ground. "Now has been corrupted by a darkness unimaginable to us. Good intentions don't always lead to good outcomes.", Josh nodded his head silently. They headed east towards the park as the sun darkened. The cold wind blew against his skin, giving him chills. The massive crater was astonishing. The black tendrils were laid all across the hole, glowing dimly. Marcus and Josh slowly slid down, their eyes darting around them. Inside the lab, the portal shone brightly. A feeling of dread filled Josh's mind. The tendrils were wrapped around the portal, pulsing. Powering up the rail gun, it beeped loudly. Marcus squeezed the trigger tightly. "It's been such a long time, *Marcus.*", Marcus froze. The voice sent chills through his body. Josh stepped back towards the portal; his hands were defensive. "I'm really digging the new hair color. Fits my suit well.", Stardust chuckled. Marcus lowered the gun, turning to face the being. He smiled, reaching his hand out. Stardust smiled back at him, shaking his hand. Josh watched in horror in the back of the room. His forehead was in a deep cold sweat. Mind spinning, trying to wrap his head around this. "I'm sure he won't be an issue?", Stardust asked, nodding towards Josh. Josh felt the cold wall against his body, scrambling to the corner. "He never even expected a thing.", Marcus laughed, stepping towards Josh. His hands were clammy, eyes clouded. His torn jacket was tugged on, he swung his arms trying to break loose of the impossible grip. His heart sank. The echoing of distant screams danced louder to his ear. The cold marble floor slid under him as he scratched at it. His hopes lessened with each inch he edged closer to his death. Their laughs taunted at him; their dark grins pierced at his bones. The tentacles wrapped tighter around his arms, dragging him closer. His screams rang through the walls as his vision whirred around him. The wind blew hard at his skin. With a thump, Josh hit the ground hard. The cold dirt sent a chill down his cheek. He raised his head, looking up at the dark sky. The cold tears poured down his face. His quiet weeping was the only sound in the dim void.

The sun darkened further. The eclipse shrouded the desolate city into pure darkness. Max peered out the shattered window, trying to make use of his flashlight. Stepping out of the building, his eyes scanned his surroundings. In a flash, his feet rushed towards the next building. The flashlight waved violently, briefly shining on the old torn flag. Burnt, the holes ruined the stripes. Max dove through the door landing on the cold hard floor. His hands were bleeding, the open scars letting out the deep black blood. It oozed onto the floor. Max shifted, lifting himself to the mahogany table. He grunted, the scar on his chest still an open wound. His eyes studied the room. The glass walls were covered in blood. The elevator lights flickered. The door silently opened. His feet guided him towards the elevator. Cold sweat began to pour down his forehead, soaking his torn shirt. The elevator lights flickered again, the door closing in as he entered. It let out a chime before the cables shifted upward taking him to the third floor. His hands were formed into fists. The elevator abruptly stopped, letting out a final chime. Its door opened slowly, revealing the dark office. He gasped, shining his light at the corpse. Her hands were cut clean off, her mouth was agape. Max knelt down. He lightly closed her eyelids before standing back up. The creaking emitted quietly, bringing Max back to his defensive mode. He raised the flashlight, it's beams shining on the figure in the office chair. His eyes tried to recognize the man. "We've expected you'd be back.", The figure's voice was clear. "James?", Max's voice was full of confusion. His shoulders tensed up; the flashlight slightly shifted. "It's been a while...Max. Quite a lot of things changed while you've been *missing*.", James spoke, adjusting his position. "I truly hope you see to our cause. The beautiful nature of the ascension of humanity.", Max slowly backed up, the realization settling in. "So, understand this. It's nothing personal. It's just...*business*.", Max watched as the man rose from the chair, the tendrils rose from under the desk. Max's legs turned to jelly. His knees buckled. He tried to run, tried to escape but his body was frozen. The lights flickered on in the office, revealing the grotesque figure in its glory. James stepped forward from the desk, smiling. The tendrils began to wrap around his chest. He squirmed trying to get free. They pushed his mouth open before slithering inside Gasping for air, his vision blurred. He looked up at James who laughed, watching the man struggle. The anger inside him swelled, the memories flooding in. All the pain, suffering and death surfaced in his thoughts. Then, he finally broke. James screamed loudly, stumbling back. The tendrils retracted out of his mouth, burning violently. Max felt the rush of air enter his lungs, bringing him back to the action. His eyes were wide with rage. With every step, his body burned with power. In one punch, James went flying across the room. He hit the glass window, cracking it. Max stepped closer, ready to beat the man to death. He cracked his knuckles. "Games, Mr. Burrows. That's all it is with you. The continued cycle of life and death. Yet, when offered a way to break this cycle. You spat in God's face. Only a fool would be oblivious.", Max spun around. Marcus faced him. His hands were stained with blood. Max stepped back, quite confused. "Marcus...? No...", Max trailed off. "Look around! Are you blind to the destruction around you? He's just using you! Once he's done, he'll just wipe you from existence.", Max tried to plead with the man. His hands shook violently. "Lord Stardust would never do such heinous acts! He is the key to our ascension. To become something greater. Something your father dreamed of.", Marcus explained, his eyes were glazed over. Max clenched his fists, "You know nothing about my father.", Max spat. Marcus let out a chuckle, shaking his head. "Such a fool. Your father would be disappointed in you.", Max let go, he let out a war cry. Charging towards Marcus, he swung punches at the man. Marcus dodged before slamming Max through the floor. Max hit the bottom floor with a crunch, his spine was shattered. Paralyzed, Marcus and James dragged him across the marble floor. His head hit the concrete stairs, bouncing up and down. Outside, the eclipse still shadowed the sun. His head continued to hit the hard basalt road as he was dragged along. It bled, leaving a trail in the darkness. After what felt like a lifetime of headaches, his captors finally stopped. The familiar scent of liquor filled his nostrils. The quiet echoing began to ring at his eyes. His heart sank to the floor. The concrete floor was cold against his skin. He felt his legs lift. His fingers felt the indented marks in the concrete. He held on, fingers bleeding. They yanked harder, stretching his legs. The screams echoed louder as he scratched at the floor, holding on to anything he could. Sliding closer, his legs felt the cold touch of the portal. "Too bad you couldn't even save Sophia.", James taunted, laughing as Max edged closer to the portal. Like a rock, Max stopped sliding. His hands shuddered with anger. Marcus pulled hard, ripping the concrete floor from under Max. But Max didn't move. His hands pulsed; his body shook. The ground began to vibrate before shaking uncontrollably. "No more.", Max spoke quietly. "What was that, *mortal?*", Marcus laughed. "No more games!", Max shouted. He moved swiftly, his hand ripping James's heart instantly. The laughter stopped. Marcus froze with fear as Max crushed the heart, the blood splattering everywhere. In a flash, Max tore the other man's head clean off. Tossing the head into the portal, he smiled. Stepping outside the laboratory, the eclipse was fading away, beaming rays of light onto the dead city. In the distance, the ground shook abruptly. The massive monstrosity tore through the city, rampaging. Max looked down at his hands, once a pale tan now a dark shade of black. It seemed to slowly spread onto his arms, the eerie glow of his veins was visible in the dim daylight. He darted quickly towards the massive entity; his eyes full of determination.

Stardust levitated across the destroyed city. He smiled at his creation, ravaging in the distance. This world, this dimension was all a game to him. Part of the endless cycle he'd created for himself. His eyes gazed at the fading eclipse, smiling. Glancing at his golden watch, he nodded. The transformation was almost complete. He could only dream of what he'd become soon. The fantasies of his sheer power expanding further pleased his mind. After decades of imprisonment, his goals would be met. No more limitations of a puny god but a supreme overlord of corruption. Stardust admitted to himself that toying with Max was pointless but he truly enjoyed destroying everything he'd had loved. Just like Max's father did to him. He could see it now. His power wielding infinite universes, his image imprinted in the very fabric of reality. Snapping out of his daydream, the monstrosity roared. It's massive tentacles flung wildly. *"I suppose the hero is here to save the day."* He lowered himself down, observing Max struggling to fight the beast. The man's skin was a deep black, his eyes were a dark green. Stardust ascended up in the air, the chills shuddering through his shoulders. Shaking his head, he pushed his worries to the back of his mind. The eclipse was nearly completed. His watch ticked quietly. *"Almost there."*, Gazing back at the battle, Stardust watched Max slam the beast to the ground with ease. The loud roaring vibrated the ground as the beast rose up, towering over Max. Stardust laughed, his hands clasped together. His watch beeped quietly, flashing. Stardust couldn't contain the burst of joy. *"It's time."*, He whispered.

Max rolled across the dirt, groaning. It's screams ruptured his eardrums. The giant shadow covered him in darkness. The heat of its body radiated off prickling at his skin. Wind whistling, its massive tendrils crashed down on Max repeatedly as he was pounded into the ground. His bones cracked; the agony was unbearable. He didn't dare to move nor could he. Each blow knocked the breath out of his lungs. The tears began to flow down his cheeks. His silent weeping was briefly interrupted with a crunch to his legs. The feeling had left a while ago, but as he looked down at his detached legs, he just felt disappointed. The monstrosity finally stopped beating at him, hovering over him with a sneering demonic laugh. His mortal enemy descended to the ground with ease, lightly touching the dirt. The man's suit was in perfect condition, not a single particle of dust. Max could hear his footsteps edged closer. Max's heart whimpered; his thoughts were begging to die. "Losing everything is hard at first.", He sensed the man's hatred through his voice. Max's eyes flooded with bloody tears running down his cheek. "But you will understand with loss...", Stardust paused, his eyes gazing at the chaos. "Opens new beginnings.", Vibrations shook through his shattered spine, his quiet moans of pain were covered by the loud shaking. Stardust began to ascend into the orange sky, the rays of the sun beamed down on him. Max watched in horror as his nemesis glowed in the daylight. The monstrosity shifted above him, slowly shrinking down into ashes. Max shielded his eyes as the glow blinded him. His hands slowly lowered down; his mouth was agape. Heart racing, his mind went into overdrive. Arms clawing at the mud, he dragged himself away slowly. His head dragged against the shattered glass, piercing into his skin. Max didn't dare look behind him, all he could do was crawl and try to hide. The ground pulsed harder, slowly dragging him back to the epicenter. The wind began to blow hard, fragments of glass buzzed past his head. His fingernails were covered with dirt, they held deep. His legs began to raise up as the wind blew harder, whipping at his skin. Fingers beginning to slip, his heart raced to push them down. Fumbling, his body slipped. Max's left hand held tightly, one by one slipping. His pinky finger bent, slowly slipping out of the small dent. The wind tore at him violently, his hands were flailing. Then, he stopped dead still. The wind stopped. Everything froze, even the glass fragments in the air. Eyes opened; his heart sank further into his stomach. "Just kill me already!", Max screamed at the shadowy figure in front of him. "You haven't broken yet.", Its voice echoed, chilling Max to the bone. Max fell to the ground, bones snapping in half as he laid there. His eyes glazed up at the orange sky. The smell of roses filled his nostrils, bringing a faint smile to his face. The shadow covered his view, as he sighed quietly, readying himself to die. Her face was stunningly gorgeous, her beautiful green eyes looked down at him. "Sophia...", Max choked, his eyes lighting up. "My poor dear, what have you gotten yourself into?", Max tried to speak, his voice was hoarse. Her fingers pressed down on his lips, silencing him. "It's time to go, love.", Her voice was soothing, soft like silk. Max felt his eyes shudder. His breathing was erratic. She reached out her hand, smiling. Max struggled to move, he watched as her hand shifted slightly. "It could be me and you, forever Max.", Her voice was a bit strained now, losing the soft and warming touch. "All you have to do is to take my hand.", Max felt his hands slowly reach towards her, embracing her offer. His hand locked in with hers as she gently lifted him up off the ground. His body began to heal rapidly, the bones fusing together. Max rose, his eyes settling on hers. Sophia stuttered, stumbling back. "Forgive me. My love.", The glass shard was embedded into her stomach. The dark blood poured out as she screamed loudly, lowering pitch by the second. Max watched her collapse onto the ground, fading away into a cloud of darkness. Lifting his hands, Stardust spun past him, slicing his side. Max didn't move an inch. Stardust swung past him, as Max grabbed the man. His hands were wrapped around the man's throat. Rising off the ground, the god struggled to free himself from Max's grip. Max's eyes burned with rage, his hands were black as night. He rose faster, higher until stopping hundreds of feet above the city. "No more power.", Max then pummeled the god into the ground, beating him to death. Stardust didn't move an inch as the god bled. Max lifted his hands again, the world shifted around him, distorting itself. He then began to beat Stardust senseless again. "Why..would you destroy your own world. To defeat me?", Stardust whimpered. "It is the only way.", Max roared before ripping God's body into pieces. His hands were stained with blood, tears rolling down his cheek. His eyes began to gaze at the chaos around him, the slow realization settling in. "What have I become?", Max spoke, hinting of regret in his voice. Max felt himself collapse. His eyes met his nemesis one final time, the man smiling back into his soul. The world fractured around him; reality fell from the sky in pieces. The laughter echoed in his ears quietly, reminding him. With one final breath, he braced himself. Hands clenched; the world shifted under him. The quick darkness s

Max felt the cold touch linger across his skin. His hands were restrained. The straps were tight. He shifted in the bed, trying to get free. The doctor quickly entered the room, his face was full of relief. "I'm glad you're awake, Mr. Burrows. It's been quite some time.", Max stared at the man, confused. He tried to speak, but no sound came out. "I'll make sure to notify the guests.", The doctor exited the room quickly. Max struggled violently, trying to free himself of the straps but it was no use. Two figures entered the room, a man and a woman. Max froze. His hands balled in defense. "Oh, I was so worried you were never coming out of the coma.", Her amber eyes were full of joy. Tears ran down his face, his hands trembled. His heart raced, glancing at the man next to her. Their hands were latched together. Max began to rock the hospital bed violently, trying to scream. "Doctor, he's having a heart attack!", The woman called out. She left the room quickly, but the man with the suit stayed. His fedora was tipped, concealing his face. "I'll see you soon.", The word came out of his mouth, torturing Max. He quickly left the room, leaving Max to his imprisonment. Heart racing faster, his vision blurred as the machine beeps louder. Footsteps rushed in the room, the faint voices of the doctor with an urgent voice. Their voices slowly faded as he wriggled back and forth with no effort. With a quick prick to the shoulder, his eyes shuddered violently before slamming shut. The word rang through his mind over and over, increasingly growing louder with each time. The cold wind blew hard across him, feeling himself being carried by it. The dim light peered at his eyes. His eyes opened; the voices whispered behind him. He inhaled the wonderful scent of roses, bringing a sense of familiarity that he couldn't place. He smiled, reaching for his collapsed flag in his backpack. "What do you think we should call it?", The man asked beside him. "I think.", Max spoke, peering at the tall waterfall. "I think we should call it, Silent

Falls.",

The End.

Made in the USA
Columbia, SC
05 August 2022